A NOVEL BY

Anthony Creach

Street Life
P U B L I S H E R S

Library of Congress Cataloging-in-Publication Data; Creach, Anthony

CROOKED: a novel/by Anthony Creach

For complete Library of Congress Copyright info visit;
www.streetlifepublisherz.com

ISBN 13: 978-0-983-44093-2

P.O. Box 2112
Minneapolis, MN 55402

Cover and interior design by www.MarionDesigns.com
Editing by Gail Lennon

Acknowledgments

First and foremost, all praises to God, my savior of all the stars, the moon and world. Without your love and unselfishness, none of this would be possible. You gave me a piece of the bottom only to have me humble myself graciously as I head for the top. Thank you for loving me and not giving up on my sinful but changing everyday soul.

My dad, father, guardian, and best friend, Thank you for the strength, the dominance, and the leadership. You've inspired and influenced me throughout my life. Without your guidance and fatherly support, this dreading and agonizing road I just traveled would've broken me like empty beer bottles. When I didn't know who to trust or which way to go, once again you pointed me in the right direction. I love you for loving me first.

My brother Jamie, my one and only TRUSTED AND TRUE BLOODLINE in this whole world. I'm so relieved that you chose to not follow in my footsteps by picking up all the awful and untamed shit that got my ass a life sentence at the end of my run. I'm very proud of you for getting your life together and being that man and father to your beautiful babies. A REAL MAN NEVER FOLD like a bad dealt hand when it comes to stepping up and taking care of his responsibilities and duties for his family. Forever together, we can conquer any obstacles that get in our way. I love you and this is just the beginning.

Grandma, you're the queen and royal jewel to our family. Without your motherly love and ambitions for your own children, our generation after them wouldn't be as strong as as it is now. Through all of our ups and downs, twists and turns, right and wrongs, you've stayed by each one of us. Showering us with your unconditional and forgiving love, like raindrops from the heaven above. I love you for taking part in my creation and watching me blossom like the rose that you are.

The entire CREACH family, I love ALL of you. We some special muthafucka's in our own special muthafucken way. We like one of a kind and I am absolutely proud to be a part of this clique. Aunt Arlene and Uncle Jerry, I love you two dearly. Uncle Noopy, get your music to someone who will put your shit on wax, Marc (it's cool), Sherry (praying for you), Ed, Freddy, Big Ollie, Jim Bone, Bertha, Loretta, Lil Ollie, Jonathon, Lil Tony, Retta (I ain't forgot you), Lamont and Tiffany, I love you all.

My wonderful and beautiful cousin, Kris. I love you like a baby sister and I apologize for not being able to watch you grow up into the strong and unwavering young woman that you are now. However, I'm here now and I'm not going anywhere. Please stay focused on your school and career and let everything else fall into place. Believe me, it will. Thank you for everything.

My nieces and nephews who are the princesses and princes of my life. India, London, and Brooklyn, I love you three and I do this for y'all. Know your importance in life, that is to be strong, god fearing, educated and independent black women. Always carry yourselves like queens. My two nephews, Jaron and Jordan, stay sharp, conscious, unmarked, and consistent. Remember to always watch over your sisters and to be that sword and shield for each other.

The second place I call home, BEAVER FALLS, PA YO! WHAT UP, BABY! This shit is for yall too. There is know way I could forget about my family and friends down there. You nigga's will always hold a special part in my life. Much respect!!! Mr. Westcott, DAMN! I don't know how I could have made it without your helping me. You saw the determination and drive in me that has allowed me to achieve what I have. I thank you very much for all that you have done for me. You are a true friend. What up T Drake, Big Chip, da Freak, Mari, Max Cool V, Reese Shawny Mo, Slap, Ron C Jason Wright, Ice, Ebony, Narketa, Lo, Cheese, Jersey Drive, 250, Buster, Pretty Rickey, Mack Man, Itty Bitty, Melbo, Dee, Prince, Roxy, Dave Thomas, Westside Weez, Mark, Young Phil, Big Bill, Todd money, Tutu, P-Zo, Big sauce, Mel El, John Woods, 5-5, Hitman, Terri (Thank you so much), Sweetman (I ain't forgot you), Geno, D Man, Detroit Dirty, Fred Ward, Lil Shawn Marcus, Baby Lou, Ken Blackshaw (What up OG), Dez, Fat ass man (Told you), Greg, Cory, Rance, Rudy, Ryan, Goober, Dink, Nez, Stacy, Goldie, Snoop the king (keep spiting fire), Tall Walt (what up cuz), Short, Tank, Tone, Banks, Chuck F, NYC Tone, Dro, Boo Boo, Hummy (keep ya head up cuz), Bruce, Boo John, Mike Jones,

Janaia (hey baby), Tara, Davy D, Chink, AP, Bud, Goggy, Fat Dame, Cam, Mr. Wilford, The fucken parole board for letting a nigga go, J-Bone, Stone, Young Head, Rob, Rome, Cringle, Spade, Click, Pretty Paul, Stretch, Curt, Ren, Shawn, Wynn (St. Clair), JFK(get dat $$$), Pete, B.Clouds (good lookin), the whole midwest, the D-Boys, Jack boys, and my nigga D Houston,

Finally, to the ruthless and scandaless city that I call home, EAST CLEVELAND muthfucken Ohio. We some rotten as nigga's. Ain't no place like this in the world. I love where I come from and what I represent. Let's not continue to allow for our crime infested neighborhoods and high unemployment rates detour our blessings that's lined up for all of us. It don't matter where we come from in life, it only matters where we tryin to go. Let's believe in that and work hard to get there together.

All my page nigga's still holding the block down, keep watching for those fake nigga's who look like us, dress like us, talk like us, but ain't US. Fella's World!!!

To the whole city of Cleveland, I love my city and without some of you foul ass nigga's, I wouldn't have a story to tell. Shout out to Big Chew, Bear, Blacc ass Skeet, 350, ugly boo, all my nigga's off Hayden & Euclid rocking leathers, stacking cheddar and blowing holes in nigga's feathers. To all my St. Clair & Lakeshore Homeboys tucking, ducking, and causing mad rukus. To all my nigga's off the 10-5 block holding it down keeping the police busy. To my superior cats, riding dirty with no thoughts of getting clean. Shout out to my kinsman, 131st, & 93 nigga's totting heavy metals, puffing on that kush. To my Harvard, union, & miles nigga's placing dice bets while my hustling honeys boosting and passing bad checks. Shout out to all those nigga's off Woodland, MLK, & buckeye getting dat dirty $, all up and down 55th, WHAT UP! My project nigga's down the way collecting chips and rolling mad thick, to my Wadepark, Hough, & 79th nigga's pushing white packs & Wu sticks. Shout out to my Cedar & Quincy nigga's bugging, thugging, and mean mugging. To my garden valley nigga's totting and heavy blowing passing on that Reggie bush. To the whole Westside of the city, up & down Clark, Lorain, Detroit, & Dension. I can't forget my Puerto Rican family getting presidente Muerto, Que Pasa Monicon. To all the beautiful & voluptuous women in the city that bring nigga's to they knees. To all the mom and pop stores getting their grind on, barber shops, beauty spots, hustlers of all sorts, jacks of all trades, watch for the suckas in the back, they hatin like fuck! To all the stores and magazines that carry my work, THANK YOU so much for the support. I have to thank Street Life Publishers for believing in me and giving me the chance to bring my skills to the urban readers. Good looking out Derrick and Shameka. RIP Merrill "Micky" Creach (love you), Uncle Fred, Aunt Tee, John Creach (miss you), Brian Timberlake, Chris Harris, Tracy Moore, John Harris, Rob Lee, Trone, Fish, & Pooh. The world misses you all.

All those I hurt in my past, I truly apologize to you. I was young and had no sense of direction. If you can't accept that, then fuck you! Oh yeah, Fuck you to LeBron.....U BITCH.

CHAPTER *1*

The year was 1981. The disco era had just passed. It had stormed its way through the country, leaving its mark on Afro Americans who partied hard wearing towering Afros, enormous bellbottom pants, and driving brand new, sparkling Cadillac's with fat, whitewalls.

These sights were the every-day highlights for me, growing up in the city of East Cleveland off Page Avenue and Euclid. For those who weren't hip, this was an undersized black city that sat in the middle of Cleveland. This bankrupt city had its own dishonest mayor, crooked, racist-ass cops, and a serious crime rate as high as bigger cities across America. This undersized black city of twenty-four thousand had niggas running the streets not afraid to get that money by any means necessary. This city was known for pumping out major players in the pimp game, major dope dealers in the dope game, and major stick-up kids who would kill for major paper.

I grew up in this city. I had the impressions that head

busting, pussy advertising, and whipping fly big cars with the diamond in the back, sunroof top. Digging in the scene with the gangster lean ruled everything around a young nigga. I observed with a watchful eye, as my father and his boys ran the streets smacking the shit out of their whores if they came up short with their bread. Not that Wonder Bread for a fancy dynamic peanut butter and jelly sandwich that sat in your mother's breadbox! But that real bread that kept those silky suits close to their athletic frames. That real bread kept that mean in those nigga's steps, and that real bread that could get a nigga's shit splattered in a pissy, dim-lit hallway from a wide boy stick up.

I remember, when I was younger, I use to get wakened in the middle of the night by my father's fucking the shit out of some new female he was trying to break in to traffic that pussy for a small profit. If the loud moans, groans, and bed boards weren't waking me up, then it would be the gun shots buzzing loudly outside my bedroom window.

My father did not actually have the time to spend with a little kid and my moms wasn't in the picture at all. So, I found myself being raised by those harsh streets that cared for no one. I wasn't one of those lucky kids blessed enough to have someone take the time out to make sure that I had a decent education or to have my head on straight. I also wasn't fortunate enough to have the few peers who were in my life whisper to me that I could be the next black surgeon or black mayor to run a major black city. The only things that those old men pushed into my waxed eardrums was never to pull a gun out unless I was geared up to blow a hole in nigga's leather; never switch out no muthafuckas no matter the case. They told me to run this package across the street and promise to never look inside it. Other than that, the only positive influence I received from anyone came from Captain Kangaroo, Mr. Rodgers' Neighborhood, and Sesame Street on PBS.

On the other hand, I did have some other young cats running the streets with me who were feeling the identical sting that I endured every day. We all were living in a one-parent household, where the other parent was either lost to the adversities of the street or the prison system that housed a horde of black males and females like a parking lot full of used cars.

Growing up, me and my friends had all experienced nights without a hot meal in our small bellies resulting from the absence of our parents or the nodding off of the babysitter who was high as a kite from cans of Colt 45 brew or heroin. So, taking matters into our own gritty hands, me and my boys began to steal from neighbors who had the nerve (or stupidity) to leave their doors cracked open enough for us to slither through them like the snakes that we were becoming.

Occasionally a mothafucka would catch all of us up in a corner store, snatching and grabbing whatever we could get our filthy hands on. We would take our chances with any mothafuckas who chose to turn their heads for one split second too long.

Countless days and nights when my father would be running the streets laying his pimp down, I would be chillin' on the front stoop of my apartment building, watching the older cats push mad yellow envelopes of dope and marijuana to those whose money wasn't funny. This was my only way of learning how to approach the game head on, not allowing for the game to sneak me from behind in one of the pissy, dimly-lit hallways like a thief in the night. I wasn't going to be one of the many who got swallowed up by the boulevards because I was just in the way. Fuck dat!

At the age of twelve, me, and my best friends Cool, and Suki, were out in the streets trying to get it the best way that we could. We wanted those fresh, new Nikes and those fresh, crisp Levis that everyone was rocking. So, we started slinging nickel bags of weed in small plastic sandwich bags at school, pool halls, jumping-ass house parties, and to the older cats that held the corners up promising not to run their mouths to our parents. Damn! Thinking back that far, I wonder how in the world I could forget the summer of 1994? It was a scorching-hot summer. It was also the first time that I saw a nigga getting his shit splashed all over the ground. I learned that a revolver could solve any problems that flared up like a bad case of hemorrhoids.

Tonto was my big, Indian homie. He was more than off the hook. This nigga was straight up disconnected. I mean, I respected him, because he ran around the 'hood bringing mad havoc to all those who got in his way. He didn't give a fuck about who you was or what kind of weight you brung to the table. He just wanted to bring niggas mad doses of pain and put fear into their hearts.

On this one calm summer night, Tonto and some other cats was out in front of the building shooting dice like they did all the time. While they were gulping down a forty-ounce bottle of Old English and calling out points and bets, a tiny uproar started to fizz up.

Tonto pushed his long hair to the other side of his huge, red face after the dice had stopped bouncing around on the calm concrete. Reaching over the dice and some nigga named Space Cowboy, Tonto began to pick up the crumpled bills that sat in the grass. "Hold up, nigga. What the fuck wrong with you?" Boo Boo spoke strongly. He was the one that seen the move being shuffled on all of them. Word is, Tonto forgot his point and just tried to pick up the pot on his next roll. This crazy-ass nigga was known throughout the 'hood for pulling some wild bullshit like this. And sometimes he even got away with it because some didn't have the balls to say shit about it. However, Boo Boo had those balls that others craved

Tonto said, "Nigga, that was my point and if it wasn't, it is now. As a matter of fact, get the fuck out my face, clown-ass nigga." Tonto had the crumpled up bills in his big hands, and was stuffing them into his loose-fitting black Levi pockets. He stared at the other dudes who dared not look back at him. He then smiled at Boo Boo, while pushing his long shiny hair over his huge back, hoping and praying Boo Boo would confront him one more time so he could knock Boo Boo's teeth out his face. Not getting the static that he had hoped he would get for taking the money, Tonto then turned around and started to make his way up the block, never casting a single look behind him.

Not taking it on the chin like a bitch-ass nigga would, Boo Boo galloped up the street to face up to the Indian giant who had pocketed his bread. Boo Boo didn't care how the others wanted to play their hand. He knew, as a man, he couldn't accept that shit win, lose, or draw. Boo Boo called out, "Tonto. Hey! Tonto." As Tonto turned around, Boo Boo threw a forceful punch to the square jaw of the big giant. It had no effect on the stunned Indian.

In return, Boo Boo got a look that told him that Tonto had been waiting for this for a long-ass time. As Tonto grabbed his jaw and shook off the light sting, he started to march towards the man with the little scrawny punch. Realizing that the punch had no effect on the Indian, Boo Boo knew that some adjustments needed to be made. What happened next would change Tonto's life and mine too.

Boo Boo heaved out the snub-nosed .38 with a practiced ease that indicated he had executed this maneuver plenty of times in front of his bedroom mirror while his moms was at work. Before Tonto could comprehend that the game had changed dramatically, it was too late. The last sound Tonto heard was the sound of the gun. BANG!

The sizzling bullets pierced Tonto's reddish skin, forcing the blistering slugs into his forehead like a termite burrowing into some aged dry wood. Before Tonto realized what had taken place, part of his brain was sitting on top of a blue Chevy Impala's windshield. His big body staggered forward then backwards before plummeting to the warm concrete.

I gaped in astonishment. I couldn't believe what I had just witnessed. Everyone else who witnessed this mind-boggling moment jetted off running in all directions away from the fallen corpse. Didn't nobody want to be a witness to a nigga who had just got his shit split open like a watermelon! I decided to run as well—right towards the twitching body of the fallen Indian. I glanced at the giant chunk missing from back of Tonto's head. The nearer I got, the more I could see that he had pissed on himself and that his bowels had moved. I smelled a strong stench. See, I only got to see this type of shit on television or by someone telling a story while drinking on a bottle of warm cheap wine in the court yard of my building.

I kicked at the motionless body a few times, and then

kicked a bit harder, noticing I wasn't getting the response I would normally get from a live man. Looking around one more time to see who was watching me, I rushed his pockets and took the earnings from the game, plus the big hunting knife he wore at his side. Where he was going, Tonto sure as hell wouldn't need these things. That one saying I always heard rung true to my ears: Never bring a knife to a damned gun fight. That's why I always stayed geared up for slip ups. I wasn't going to get caught with my pants down.

CHAPTER 2

Me and Cool was chillin' in the backseat of the Acura truck with Nickels and the cat, Pete. The Nickels was getting a little bit of bread out here and he figured he knew the streets well enough to roam these dangerous mothafuckas. Yet, he had no idea what fatality was in his near future. He was about to become the victim of a wicked crime—a wicked crime that was sure to bring crocodile tears to his mother's big brown eyes.

I sat behind Nickels, bouncing the soft powder in my hands loving its pliable touch. "It feels like the weight is right. Where the other one at?" I asked.

Nickels reached under the driver's seat and pulled out the other thousand grams of coke and tossed it to me. He said, "Yo! What you going to do, playa? You going to cop this work or what? I don't feel safe sitting in the dark like this. As a matter of fact, why y'all keep shooting out the street lights over here?" Cool started laughing because he could smell the bitch oozing off this nigga. "You ain't got to worry. You in good hands around here, playboy."

Pete wasn't trying to hear none of that shit because he had heard plenty scanless stories about Page niggas and how we got down. Pete said urgently, "Yeah, that's all good. But where the money at? Let's get this shit over with before we all end up in jail tonight."

Well, this nigga was right about getting this shit over with. But, he was dreadfully wrong about niggas going to jail. Mothafuckas wasn't going to jail. They was on their way to the county morgue tonight. Hell yeah! Those niggas was about to get splashed up in this mothafucka. I was about to make it rain on a nigga's ass tonight. I reached inside my leather and grabbing the butt of the .357 long barrel so tightly that, if the gun had had a pair of lungs, I would've choked the life out of it. I then looked at Cool and gave him a Joker's smile. Play time was in full effect, baby.

I positioned the tip of the chrome barrel up against the back of Nickels' leather seat and pulled the trigger twice. BOOM! BOOM! The bullets blew through the leather seats. The two scorching slugs ripped Nickels' small chest open like a fat mothafucka on a small bag of Lay's Sour Cream chips.

Blood leaped out of the huge smoking holes in his chest cavity, splashing hard against the steering wheel and dashboard of the flashy truck. Nickels' floppy, lifeless body fell up against the horn of the steering wheel causing a loud, unwanted blare. The stage was already set as I pointed the pistol at Pete's ass that was now opening the passenger's side of the truck trying to get away from the madness I was bringing. "Bitch, where you trying to go?" I shouted at him.

Cool's Tech .9 jammed on him as he tried to push the

seat up on Pete who was trying to get away. However, fright had kicked in overtime giving Pete the strength to push the seat up off him so he could get away.

BOOM! I fired the baby cannon at Pete and watched the sizzling bullet destroy the top of the passenger's leather seat. The punk ass had made it out the truck and was running up the street. I fired a couple more shots through the windshield, missing him. "Damn! This nigga got away with witnessing a murder."

I was lying on the couch watching LeBron James give up on me and the Cleveland fans as we played Boston in the playoffs when my phone started screaming. It was my homie, Dave. He's was an older cat who taught me most of the shit that I knew about when it came to those streets. When it came to packing that shit, cocking that shit, and rocking that shit, Dave was the one that schooled me.

I spoke into the phone and said, "What up, baby?"
Dave said with no hesitation, "Check this out! I got something real sweet for us. I mean so damned sweet that all ya damned teeth will fall out ya mouth. That type of sweet, nigga. Now, meet me at the Best Steak House. Yo, for real. Don't be late, cuz."

I rose from the malleable couch with the quickness of a hungry mountain lion. Dave had got my attention loud and clear and in return, I said, "Alright, I'll meet you down there in half an hour. It better be good."

It felt good to be back in East Cleveland where it all

began for me. That Page life I breathed, lived, and loved paved a road for my physical structure and mental stress that the 'hood could put on a man's brain. Shit was just inflexible for a young black man trying to make it in these uneasy times.

I pulled into the small plaza off Euclid and parked my silver Dodge Challenger in front of the restaurant that was being run by some Arabs. They had most of the stores in my neighborhood on lock. These turban-wearing, strap-a-bomb-to-your-chest muthafuckas was getting all the black man's hard-earned money, while we sat around plotting on each other's pockets instead of theirs.

Before jumping out the side, I took a quick look to my left then right to search for the jack boys who played shit tight around here. Plus, I seen Dave's Ford Fusion was nowhere in sight. After not seeing either, I got out and walked into the spot, grabbing me a table in the back where I could keep an eye on the front door. Smelling the pleasant food in the air, I decided to order something to eat. I was picking up a little appetite from the Gran Daddy Kush I smoked earlier in the day. The restaurant wasn't full to capacity, but there were enough famished people up in the spot for the owner to turn a nice profit.

After ordering a steak and egg platter, I heard the bell that sat over the entrance door rattle. DING! DING! I looked up, hoping it was Dave. Instead, it was the prettiest female I've ever seen in my life. Megan Good, who? This beautiful specimen came in with another female that was tight but nothing like the elegant one that had caught my eye and attention. "Damn!"

She looked like she had some type of Indian decent flowing through her veins with that appealing long, black, silky hair surging over her shoulders. Her skin was as flawless as a newborn baby's. Her hazel eyes told a story of their own and had a way of speaking to me without her pretty mouth parting like the Red Sea. The outfit she wore was a tight but respectful Prada black skirt with a white flimsy blouse that sat loose on top of her perfect breasts. The open Prada sandals she wore showed off her pretty toes and pedicure that I just couldn't take. Me being a straight up freak for a cute small foot, I swear I couldn't take the agony anymore. I was stuck like Chuck, gazing at her. The only reason that my gaze had to be released was because she caught me gaping her down.

I ain't never been scared of nothing in my life. But, it took me a minute to gather myself. When I was finally getting my shit together to run over to her table, I heard the bell ring once again. DING! DING! I glanced up to a wondering Dave who was looking all over for me. I tossed my hands up in the air signaling my location.

"What up, baby? My fault for taking so long, but I was caught up in a little something and no, it wasn't no pussy this time." He laughed loudly and was ready to spit his guts up on why he called me down here, 'til he seen my plate finally arriving. I pulled my plate close to me as if I was protecting it from a perpetrator and said, "What you got to tell me that's so important to get me down here?"

Staring steadily at my plate, Dave finally looked up at me with a grin and said, "That bitch Nikki done hit the damned jack pot, baby. I mean she really hit the jack pot." I tore a piece of the steak off and pushed it into my mouth while listening intensely. "She told me that there was going to be more than fifteen bricks about to be moved between some Detroit niggas and Marcus' fat ass."

I stopped eating and place my fork down not believing what I had just heard. I'd been wanting to get that fat mothafucka for a long time. I just couldn't catch the nigga slipping like I needed to. But if this was true, then it was on.

I said, "You sure, Dave? That bitch Nikki ain't playing no games is she?"

Dave slid his chair up to the table some more and said in a serious tone, "Do I play games, nigga? Hell yeah I'm sure! If I'm willing to put my own damned life on the line for this shit, you best believe that it's real. Now, what you want to do?"

His girl was good at what she did. I can't front about that. Turning us on to licks was what she did. I knew for a fact that Nikki would suck a muthafucka's dick and ass to find out where that currency was stashed at. I watched as Dave slid my plate towards him to take a piece of my steak and stick it in his greedy face as I thought. I knew for a fact that this fat nigga wasn't going to just let some cats run up in his spot like it was sweet. That would be just too easy. We was going to have to come heavy. And heavy we was going to come if it was up to me. Shrugging my shoulders, I said, "Let's do this, nigga. Get all the information down and I'll take care of getting the straps together."

With a mouth full of my steak and eggs, Dave said, "That's what I'm talking 'bout. Where Suki and Cool? We got to let these niggas know what's up." I told him that Suki had gone back to Chicago to see his family and that Cool was laying up with that nothing-ass bitch of his. Dave just shook his head. Cool's girl couldn't keep it real with him that she was feeling another cat while he was behind bars doing an eighteen-month sentence.

Me and Dave said our good-byes. Before I left the restaurant, I needed to say something to the pretty, young lady. She was sitting at the table by herself now. Her girl had stepped into the powder room. I knew this was my chance to make my move. And I had to make it count. Damn! She was fine as wine. "Excuse me, I don't tend to be rude or disrespectful, but you are sooo fuckin' beautiful." I couldn't believe that my lips had just said that. But the cat was out of the bag now and I had to roll with the punches I just dished out.

She looked me up and down with a smile then said, "Well, thank you very much. You're not bad looking yourself." I knew that I had to hurry up and shoot my shot before her girl came out of the bathroom hating and spitting salt on my game because I wasn't hollering at her.

"What's your name, baby—if you don't mind me asking?"

With no hesitation, she replied, "My name is Jasmine. What's yours?"

Keeping up the pace that we had flowing, I said, "My name is Anthony. However, my friends call me Hectic."

She giggled a child's giggle then said, "Hectic!"

Mad that I even told her that shit, I said, "Well there's a long story to that name, but maybe one day I'll be able to tell you how I got it."

I watched her go into her Prada bag. She pulled out a black card and handed it to me. "Here's my number, cutie. Maybe you'll get the chance to tell me how you got that name, Hectic."

Before I could leak another word out, I saw her friend coming out of the bathroom beaming down on us like a big sister looking after her little sister. I wanted to bounce before she made it over to us, so I said, "Well, it's been an honor talking to you and you can best believe I'll be using this number." I reached inside my pocket and pulled out a respectful size knot of money to let her know that I had a little bit of green. I placed a fifty on the table and sauntered away.

Outside, I took a nippy gaze to my left, then a nippy gaze to my right to make sure the jack boys wasn't scheming on a lick they felt was something sweet. Blowing a few holes in a nigga's Parker was straight up my alley for those who didn't believe, trust, or feel I was capable of making a nigga disappear.

Feeling relieved from the quick date, I jumped in the car. I can't front one bit. I felt kinda good because I'd met a fine-ass bitch. Then, on top of that, I was about to put that nigga Marcus' fat ass in a choke hold. Yeah! So far the day was glowing. Now all I had to do was holla at old man George.

Old man George was my man when it came to that heavy weaponry. You know what I'm saying? When it came to laying the heat down on lames, old man George had the tools to take care of it—from .22's to rocket launchers. Yeah, my nigga had enough blistering shit to take down a small county.

The time was now seven in the evening. My phone screamed that familiar scream as I pulled up to old man George's junkyard. "What's the deal?" An unfamiliar voice spoke into my phone stating, "Baby, I need you. Baby, I need you to come over here and stroke this kitty cat."

Puzzled, I asked, "Who in the hell is this?"

All I heard after that was, "See, nigga? You ain't shit. You got all those bitches in your face. You don't even know the voice of your real bitch."

It was Shantel, my damned ex, and she was mad-crazy for real. I mean some of that, thin line between love and hate crazy. I don't know why she couldn't take it that I didn't want to fuck her no more, because she wasn't trying to hear none of that. So, maybe she would hear this! I hung the phone up while she was still talking. I wasn't on it.

Sitting in front of the Junkyard, I blew the horn and within seconds four big-ass Dobermans ran to the gate showing how they enjoyed greeting people they didn't know. The fuming mutts was bouncing and jumping off the gate, while barking and slobbering all over their shiny coats. Within seconds, old man George came to the gate and with a sleight of the hand like a magician, the dogs had stopped barking.

Old man George stood looking at me with these thick-ass glasses he wore tight to his face 'til he finally recognized who I was. He then started to unchain the big gate that surrounded his fortress of junk. I pulled my car in and waited for him to hook it back up. Meanwhile, his dogs kept their eyes on my black ass and any sudden moves I tried to make that they didn't agree with.

Old man George was an old-school car "mechanic" whose smile would let you know his true age because of the limited teeth he rocked in his vacant mouth. But he was good people, just trying to get that paper like everyone else in this free world struggling with this hard economy President Bush's bitch-ass put us all in.

After wrapping the fat heavy chain back around the gate,

old man George then jumped into the passenger's seat, yelling. "Hey, boy! You still staying razor-blade sharp?"

Although talking to me, old man George was looking all around the car making sure I was the only other person beside him in the car. His behavior was understandable. Sensing that everything was cool, he finished, "What brings you around here, young'un?"

I let off a large smile as I drove by all the junk he had surrounding his house like an art gallery full of sculptures. "I want to check out a few engines you got stashed up in here. Is that cool with you?"

The old man looked me up and down a few times letting me see the Smith-'n-Wesson he had tucked in his overalls, and then gave me a toothless smile. "Yeah, you alright with me. Come on and I'll show you something real nice."

I got out of the car and walked with the old man and the four Dobermans that prayed I fucked up so they could sink their lengthy teeth into my young, black flesh. I kept my eyes on the hungry dogs as we walked into a dense garage where two men were working on a truck. Mountains of sparks were shooting over the garage like shooting stars. We turned into another room on the left, then another room on the right. I was now in the office I wanted to be in.

This room looked like some shit you would see in an executive's office building downtown. It was clean and polished with nothing but Italian leather and marble. The old man walked around his mahogany desk. Taking off those thick-ass glasses he said, "What you want, bro?" All that old-boy talk and young'un shit went flying out the window when it came to taking care of business and getting that money.

"I need some of that hot shit, George. Not no rockets or shit like that, but something that will lay a few muthfuckas down."

The old man lit up the half cigar that sat in the crystal ashtray, then walked over to the far wall and tilted a picture frame that held a picture of a black nigga and woman rocking afros in the doggy style position.

In seconds, the wall began move in a mechanical, robotic manner. At the back this rotating wall rained showers of artillery—everything a cat would love to get his hands on. There was everything from small handguns, big handguns, assault rifles, to sub machines guns, rockets, and hand grenades that would leave a psychotic killer's tongue hanging out of this mouth. The old man said, "Here!" With that, he tossed me a long black duffle bag. "Get what your money can pay for."

I ended up grabbing an AK-47 choppa, one M-16 with a hundred round drum, two P-89 Rugers, one AR-15, one Mac-11, and two chrome pistol grip pumps. We couldn't leave no witnesses to the violence we was about to mix up with these clown-ass niggas. Shit! Playtime was now in session.

CHAPTER 3

JASMINE:

I live in a moderately even-tempered suburb outside of Cleveland called, Westlake. Here, you would find your white soccer moms who drove the Caravans full of white soccer kids who loved to drink Sunny Delight and talk back to their laid-back parents. In this community, you didn't have to worry about cars riding around pumping loud music or seeing kids standing on every corner you passed trying to sell you something illegal. Here, you could sit back, relax, and love life as it breezed by like an easy-going summer's day.

Originally, I was from the Washington D.C. area raised on the southeast side of the chocolate city. I had one brother and two sisters, who were much older than I. Yet, we still continued to stay in touch as much as possible. Family truly mattered to me—especially after my parents were killed when I was sixteen years old in a brutal robbery. As I can remember, my parents were inside the corner store, purchasing a pack of Kool's and some other small items when two thugs rushed the show and robbed the place leaving not one eyewitness to their bloody madness.

That unpleasant incident changed my life forever making me want to finish high school and get into law-enforcement. I wanted to do my part in helping keep the streets safe and put those in jail who chose not to follow the rules. Those animals that killed my parents were never caught and I promised my parents up in heaven that I would do everything in my power to prevent that happening to another family.

I've been a police officer for over twelve years. I was now working undercover for the Feds in Cleveland, where I had to investigate a major drug supplier in this area.

Just a few years ago, I had been involved in another drug investigation in Landover, Maryland, where I helped drag down some very dangerous Jamaican boys. In the process, I caught one bullet in my right thigh and two more hot ones in my back that the Jamaicans had hoped and prayed would've killed my ass. God was on my side that night, leaving me to count my blessings every day for sparing my life.

I took on the job of working undercover once more because I loved the thrill of being in the middle of that underworld lifestyle of drug dealers and murders. Plus, in the end, I got to see their drug empires crumble beneath them when we knocked that ass.

As I sat on my porch, sipping a cup of coffee, I checked out the updates on a suspect named, Stanley Marcus. He was a huge drug dealer and murderer from the southeast side of Cleveland. As I could tell, he was certified as a real street criminal.

Now, my job was to get the proof that the Feds needed to nail this scumbag to the wall. Luckily, I had met a very strange, but interesting woman who was familiar with Marcus and his crew. I knew for a fact that I had to put a plan together and work this young woman to get in alone with the suspect.

Glancing up at the stars on this pretty, hushed night, my thoughts took me back to the guy I had met at the restaurant during my lunch with Gina. I won't lie. I did find him very attractive with that curly hair and light brown complexion. Yet, I never had time to do no hooking up with my girlfriends or even a man that I found stimulating to my soul. However, I was a woman and I had my needs just as a man has his. I won't lie. I do get tired of being alone and living life with no one by my side to give me the affection and loving that I knew I deserved. I prayed that this mysterious man would pick up that phone and call me to keep me company on this warm night. But 'til then, I would have to please myself as I found myself doing almost every night.

GINA:

I stood at 5'6" and weighed in at 120 pounds with my clean, chalkboard black, pretty ass. I was raised in the King Kennedy projects and was trying to do anything to make it out of these raggedy muthafuckas.

I had a healthy, six-year-old boy by some nigga who had admitted to beating up on the pussy, but claimed to never put no seed in the pussy. Shit, I had thought about calling the Maury Show to get a paternity test done on this nigga, plus to take a free trip to New York City to get my shopping on, but I changed my mind because I, too, knew 99.9999 percent that he wasn't the father.

I lived with my moms. She was slowly but surely killing herself with all the alcohol she consumed day and night. Not only was she a heavy drinker, but she was also a sleaze bucket for these neighborhood cluckers that use our small home as a trap house for the younger drug dealers in these projects.

There was always serious traffic coming and going through the apartment like the inner belt coming downtown. I was tired of the shit. I had a son who didn't need to see all this negative behavior that took place here. It wasn't something I wanted to continue to see either.

I dropped out of high school in the tenth grade because of my pregnancy. I didn't have a damned job, and to be honest, I wasn't trying to find none. I did want to go back to school and get my G.E.D. But, I had bills to pay and I had things that I wanted and needed. Why should I go back to school when all these balling-ass niggas wanted to taste my milkshake?

"Mom, hurry up out of the bathroom so I can get Jordan cleaned up."

Finally, the door burst opened. My moms scooted by as I rushed in with Jordan in my hands like a football. I was soon stopped cold by what I observed. A fiend-ass nigga was standing in the middle of the bathroom with his dick still in his ashy-ass hands. "Nigga, if you don't get the fuck out my bathroom, I swear."

The fiend's smile faded as he rushed his penis into his trousers and got out of the bathroom as quickly as he could. I cursed to myself because I hated the situation that I was in. That's why I had to do what I did to try to make it out of the projects.

On the bright side of things, I ran into a pretty nice lady a couple of weeks ago at the Laundromat. Her name was Jasmine. I did like the bitch's style and I needed to see who she was rubbing elbows with because she had a style about her that I was feeling. I figured she had to be about her business for the simple fact of the designer gear she was always parading around in. I ain't talking about no urban shit either. Her whole style and attitude wasn't from around here. With me being so damned nosey, I had to see what her angle was and if I could get in where I needed to fit in.

SUKI:

I stood in the middle of my motel room, out of breath and sweating as if I had just finished first in the running of a city marathon. I paced back and forth from the tinted motel windows back to the thin aluminum door. I was incredibly nervous—so nervous that I couldn't see or think straight anymore.

I was gripping the .44 Desert Eagle so tightly that my knuckles began to turn white. I didn't know whether to call my boys back in Cleveland or just go out of the game in a blaze of glory. I knew that I had to make up my mind and make up my mind quickly. Time was running out like minutes on a cheap cell phone.

Spinning my head towards the lumpy, plague-ridden bed that the motel expected me to sleep on, I looked at the two, full-size bags waiting for me to open them up. Their contained treasures had me in the bind that I was in now.

See, I was happy to be back in Chicago, no doubt. This is where I was from and grew up for a short time in my life. It felt good to be back around family members I hadn't seen in years. Yet, Chicago wasn't too happy to see me or any other muthafucka, in fact. Most of the people I knew and all my favorite places to be at had changed since I had moved away. Nothing remained of all that was good back then. It was now all bad.

The whole set up was just like it was back in Cleveland. Crack and gangs had run their course in yet another one of my neighborhoods and had sucked the life and love out of one more black community. This crack and gang epidemic was just like the AIDS virus on the tip of a nasty nigga's dick—contagious.

Walking around my old neighborhood on the south side, I didn't notice one damned person 'til I made my way into the Washington playgrounds. Right here is where I used to play as a youngster. It was here that my father use to do his hand-to-hand exchanges with his friends. They called me their young G.D. All the green grass and swings that once covered this park were now missing in action like a nigga's hairline who fucked with a prison barber.

Some people just didn't change in appearance no matter how much they aged. June still looked the same as when he was ten years old. Looking him up and down, I finally said, "Long time no see, nigga."

With a large grin covering his yellow face, June stared at

me for a few seconds. Then, he said, "Suki, is that's you? Damn! It's been a long time, baby. How you doing, man?" Not allowing for me to speak, he continued on, "How your moms and that pretty sister of yours? How long you back?"

Shit, I had to put my hand up in the air as if I was back in school trying to get the teacher's attention. "Damn, boy! Let me get a word or two in. I'm glad to see you too--but damn!" We both laughed and hugged each other like lost brothers seeing each other for the first time in twenty years.

After our small greetings, we both sat on a bench trying to catch up on the past "Where everybody at?" I asked.
In response, June explained to me how drugs and gang banging had changed everyone we grew up with. They were turned out on dope, serving time for dope, or out in the streets slinging dope. He told me 'bout the ones that caught bullets to the chest and skulls for claiming Folks, Vice Lords, Latin Kings, Black Disciplines, or P-Stones. He also told me 'bout the problem he was going through trying to take care of his two small children.

"I tried the job thing," he said earnestly. "I mean, I left the streets alone to take care of my seeds, man. My baby momma out in streets turning tricks, while popping those damned blue and red dolphin pills. It's been hard on me."

I sat listening. I couldn't believe what I was hearing from my childhood friend. He used to sleep over at my crib on the weekends, and sometimes on the weekdays when his mother was out in the streets drunk as a skunk to the point she couldn't find her way home.

I knew my boy was struggling out on these cold boulevards and so was I to be honest. I was requesting and praying to catch me a nigga up here slipping. To be frank, that was my main reason for coming back up here. I never had a problem taking my show on the road and cracking a few heads open like coconuts. I needed some dead presidents in these fruitless pockets of mine. With all the niggas rolling around here with pockets full of cash, I refused to not be a part of it.

"I ain't trying to be funny or nothing. But, why you ain't hit none of these niggas up yet? These nigga's out here living good, while you sitting around here broke as hell. You complain about having no paper, but the shit sitting right in front of your mug!"

June was about to put a cigarette between his lips when he said, "I've thought about taking some of these niggas up top, but I never did it. I just been scared, man. I ain't gon' lie. I ain't never done no shit like that before."

As I sat listening to this man complain, my eyes shifted to a pack of young niggas strolling through the park looking up to no good. I could tell the young cats was Gangster Discipline by the way their hats twisted on their peanut-shaped heads.

June pulled the cigarette back out of his mouth and said, "I know this nigga on the Westside getting it. I believe he lives with his moms. But I know for a fact that he got that spread. I just never had the balls to get the nigga."

That was all I needed to hear. This was my cup of tea down in Cleveland. Why hustle when I can take yo shit?

For a couple of days, me and June followed this young kid around the city as he picked up and dropped bags off at a house on the Westside in large doses. Not having the patience to continue to sit and watch this action for one more day, I decided it was time to get paid, "Hey, we getting this clown tonight. Soon as this nigga drop that shit off, we busting up in the back door."

June said, "You sure your plan going to work? I mean, I don't want shit to go wrong."

I sat back looking at June and had second thoughts on taking this lame with me. A nigga had to have a cold heart to get down the way that I did and this one sure in the hell gave off a funky vibe that his heart was lukewarm.

I questioned him, "You scare or something?"

June tried his hardest to harden his face and voice, "Hell naw! I ain't scared. I was just thinking."

I gave him a stare one more time, then put the car in gear and pulled out into the street saying, "Then stop just thinking and get ready to get this cream."

It was six in the evening. The sun was still beaming down on the city of Chicago and the people who chose to sit in the eighty-degree weather. Me and June sat in the rusted-out Nova waiting for the final drop off while listening to DJ Timbuck 2 mix some of the hottest hip hop together like a hot pot of New Orleans gumbo.

I knew no one was in the house other than some old lady and I hoped I wouldn't have to unleash no slugs on this old hag. Didn't no one want to shoot an old black woman, for real. But, let it be known: I would if it came down to her old ass and that money. I'd scalp her old shit back with no second thoughts. I swear I would. Hopefully, things would go smoothly and unnoticed to the neighbors sitting on their porches and kids playing tag football in the middle of the street.

I looked over to June and I could tell that this nigga was scared. "You cool, nigga?" I asked him.

June responded, "Yeah, I'm slick. Let's just get this shit

over with because the nigga just pulled up." I looked over. There was that white Ford Temple with the passenger's window taped up with plastic. He was just pulling up. We both sat watching him doing his ritual grabbing a few bags from the car and whisking them into the house. A few minutes later, he reappeared toting one large bag. He jumped back into the smug he was pushing. After the Ford Temple pulled off, I pulled my car out into the alley and jumped out.

I took the safety off the meaty .44 and said, "Let's go get this paper."

We both made it to the back porch and with no hesitation. I gave the door a hard kick, knocking the wooden door off its hinges. BOOM! We busted straight in, waving the pistol around like a madman ready to lay something down. I caught a glimpse of the old lady scampering into the living-room. Giving a small chase, I screamed out, "Where you trying to go, grandma? Get your old ass over here."

She started screaming at me, "What the fuck you want? Who the hell is y'alls?"

I calmly told her, "Grandma, on some real shit. Sit your old ass down on this couch. Be still and won't nothing happen to you. But if you keep screaming like you lost your damned mind, then I'm going to lose my damned mind too and blow your brains across this room. Now, how you want to do this?"

That old lady understood me loud and clear. I took a peek into the dining-room. I saw the two bags sitting next to the dining-room table. "Watch the old lady and if she moves pop her old ass," I told June.

Before marching into the other room to grab hold of the black bags, I looked at the old lady and gave her a nice wink and smile.

While watching over the old lady, who looked to be in her early seventies, June started quavering with the chunky blue steel .38 in his sweaty palms. The old lady sat looking at June. Realizing that there was a tab of bitch flowing in his veins like white blood cells she said, "You know what? You ain't nothing but a bitch boy and when my grandson finds out you took his money, he gon' cut your little dick off and stick that little muthafucka in your mouth." She then gagged up something foul from deep in her throat and spit it at June's feet in disgust. Watching the slimy green slob splash next to his retro Jordan's, June got irritated and jumpy at the same time, forcing him to lose his cool as if the old lady was the one holding him at gunpoint.

From where I was at, I could hear all the commotion. But, before I could make it back into the living-room to calm shit down, the damage was already done.

POP! POP! POP! "Oh shit. What the fuck?" I gasped. Rushing into the living-room as quickly as I could, I was brung to a halt by the sight of the old lady stretched out across the couch with three smoking holes in her plump but fragile frame.

Two bullets had caught the old lady in the chest right above her long and sagging breast, while the other bullet she took to the side of her wrinkled face. It ripped a piece of her jaw off. I couldn't believe what I was looking at. "What the fuck you doing? Why you shoot her?"

June stood looking dumb, the smoking gun in his hands, and said, "She spit on me and on top of that, she said her son was going to cut my dick off and shove the shit in my mouth. So I shot the old bitch."

I swear I wanted to shoot my lifelong friend right in his head and leave his dumb ass next to the old lady. But, instead, I ran to the living-room front window and noticed people looking back up at the house. "Fuck." Grabbing both bags with one swift move, I found myself in the backyard racing towards the old Nova at top speed.

As I got to the car, I could hear a pair of sirens in the background, getting closer with every second I waited for June to get into the car. I wanted to waste June's blood the same damned way he did that old lady. But time wouldn't permit me to. I knew I had to get the fuck away from this murder scene.

As I turned out of the alley to hit in the side streets, I observed a patrol car turning down the street the house was on. Living in these types of conditions everyday in the city of Cleveland, I knew how to keep my cool the whole time others would've been jerky—jerky like this bitch-ass nigga June was. I told him, "Shut the fuck up!"

I continued to roll 'til we got three city blocks away from the robbery-turned-homicide. As I pulled up behind a Caravan with some little, ugly, fat, white kid making all these dumb-ass, funny faces at me, I noticed a police car sitting right behind me. The patrol car didn't have its bubble lights flashing. But, my survival wits told me that this image wasn't right at all.

June had noticed my discomfort and spun around to see the cops on our asses. This sent him into a frenzied mode. "Oh shit, we going to jail!" he ranted. "I knew I shouldn't have fucked with you, man. Shit!"

I couldn't believe what I was hearing from my homeboy. But, before I could speak up or confront this ho-ass nigga, the light turned green on me. Right when my foot hit the gas pedal to make a smooth getaway, the cops' sirens started blaring and roaring like a full-grown lion. Mashing on the gas while jumping in and out of traffic like a maniac, I was fully aware that June had frozen up on me. This forced me to grab my hammer.

Without shilly-shallying, I pulled the trigger. POW! The stray shot hit June in his side just missing his kidney. While keeping my eyes on the road, I said, "Nigga, jump yo punk ass out the car or I'll pop yo ass again."
June was clasping the smoking hole in his side trying to hold all the blood seeping out. He wailed, "Suki, you shot me. Why you shot me, man?"

I guess this nigga thought I was playing. So, I pulled the trigger again to aim for his head this time. POW!

The first bullet whizzed past him, taking out the passenger's window. So, I tried again. POW! The second bullet caught him in the top of his left shoulder and not his damned head that I was aiming for. His eyes grew big as twenty-four-inch rims as he sat screaming and crying. He knew that death was around the corner and it was coming for dat ass. However, he did get the message because he cracked open the car door while I was doing about forty, and leaped out smacking hard against an F150 parked in front of a furniture store. THUMP!

The car door stood wide open as I came to a four-way intersection packed with vehicles. Deciding to bust a quick right, I hit the brakes and watched the car fishtail to the left forcing the passenger's door to close on its own and push the rest of the loose-fitting glass into the car with me. I mashed the gas down a side street. The police car was still on me like a big fat fly on top of a steaming pile of shit.

I knew I had to get away or I was going down for two

homicides I wasn't trying to catch. Looking back into the rearview mirror, I noticed another police car and I knew soon there would be many more joining the pack.

I busted a quick left, scarping the old Nova against a parked Navigator. Not one bit did it keep me from easing off the gas. I peeped out at the railroad tracks up in front of me. I heard the train's horn blaring in the background over the sirens and hot engine inside the Nova. It was about fifty yards away. As I got closer to the tracks, I could see the muzzle of the train coming up on my right. I punched the gas more and thought if I could beat this train then I might have a chance of getting away. If not, then going to jail for life would be the least of my worries.

I took one more glance out the rearview and seen the cops still on my ass. I knew I had no choice but to do what my crazy ass was thinking about doing. I looked to my right and seen the engine of the machine moving fast, daring anything to get in its way. I hit the tracks, busted through the crossing rails and witnessed the Nova flying through the air. The Nova landed with such a force that I hit my head on the roof of the car and cracked my neck. I held my breath and closed my eyes and prayed that I wouldn't get smashed to pieces by the heavy, irritated train.

The car smashed hard to the earth on the other side of the tracks, leaving me feeling lucky and alive. It was all good 'til I started to lose control of the rusty, ass car. The Nova jumped and bounced around on the hot pavement like a child bouncing a ball. It smacked hard into a parked car then a light pole. I thumped my head hard against the steering wheel and made a deep gash over my left eye. But, I knew I had to suck up the pain and get out of the car before the police got over the tracks. Reaching into the backseat, snatching up the bags, I turned around and took my chances with this alley right in front of me.

CHAPTER 4

JASMINE:

I had just gotten off the phone with Anthony and I felt excellent since I was getting the chance to see him for the second time. Maybe this man could insert some flavor into my boring-ass life. God knows that I desired it. First, I needed to meet with my boss in a secluded area—several warehouses in the flats.

I sat in my Honda Accord and waited for the black Crown Victoria to come to a complete stop before jumping out of my own vehicle. As I marched across the street to approach the car, I could see my boss' fat, pink face taking up most of the driver's side window. Leaping into the car, I greeted him, "Hello, Petro."

Petro took his profession as seriously as the next officer. He had been on the same job for over thirty years. "Hello, Jasmine. Have you got any information yet from the hoodrat girl that you met?"

I turned my head towards the window to look at the warehouses; trying not to laugh in his face about the name he called the young girl. After getting myself together, I said, "No, not yet. But I'm working on her and as soon as I find something out, I'll let you know what the …hoodrat said."

Petro grabbed his cup of Starbuck's coffee and said, "Well, I've got some very interesting news for you involving Marcus. I hear that there is supposed to be some big drug deal going down with him and some Detroit boys in a few days. One of our thousands of snitching informants told the office yesterday. Now I don't know how true this is, but…" Taking a sip of the straight, black coffee, he continued on, "I need for you to shut this operation down before they get a chance to put those drugs on our streets. More drugs, more money. More money, more homicides. This already-torn-apart city doesn't need that."

The pressure was all on me and I was ready to take on the responsibility. I loved when the ball was in my hands at the end of the game because I loved taking the last shot just like Kobe Bryant. I considered myself to be a clutch shooter when it came down to it.

"Well, me and Gina are supposed to hook up. I'll be next to Marcus in no time," I told him. Petro seemed to believe in me. We engaged in some other small chit-chat before I got out of his car and headed back to mine.

I sat in my car with the windows down, allowing the fresh air to smack against my skin as I thought how I was going to get Gina to run her mouth. Believe me! That's all she did. She could talk a muthafucka straight into a coma. But, to get her to say what I needed to hear was a different thing. I grabbed my phone and gave the girl a call.

HECTIC:

Thoughts of Jasmine came to my mind like my favorite slow song. I was really feeling shorty and I wanted to get close to that. So, I used the number that she had gave me and asked her if I could take her out tonight. She tried to play that shy role. But, I could tell in her giggle that she was feeling my style. I soon found myself writing down her address.

Getting out of the shower rushing to figure out what to put on, I heard my phone scream out the loud ring.

"Hello!" I heard a familiar voice on the other end that sounded distraught. "Hectic, I'm in a muthafucka jam, nigga and I need your help."

I still couldn't figure out who it was, so I said, "Who is this?"

The strange voice shot back, "Nigga, its Suki and shit real up here in the Chi."

I sat on the bed and said, "What you talking 'bout?"

Not wasting time by saying what the problem was, Suki said, "Hec, on some real shit, I ain't got time to be explaining nothing right now. I just need for you to send somebody up here to get my ass."

There was no possible way that I could turn my back on my people. Loyalty was a big thing with me and a big part of the way that I was raised up in these streets. I could tell by the way he was breathing into the phone that shit was serious. "Okay, I'll send someone to get you at the bus station downtown. Call me back in ten to twenty minutes. I got you, baby."

I hung the phone up and called my girl who was more thug than some of these wanna-be Muppet-ass niggas out there in these streets, playing games. My girl agreed to do it for me and I told her I would have something for her when she got back to Cleveland.

After getting fresh to death, I made my way over to pick up Jasmine's sexy ass. I blew the horn only once. Jasmine came out the house looking stunning. I mean she was so damned fine that I was amazed that she didn't start another million man march right behind her well-shaped ass.

When she finally got into the car, she instantly had it smelling like rose petals and the month of May. The light, sweet smell that soared in the air tickled my nose hairs and unconsciously made me lick my lips like LL Cool J. "Damn! You smell good as hell, girl," I told her.

Jasmine smiled showing her pearly whites and said, "Thank you. You smell good too."

Trying not to blush at her comments and hold my shit in check, I pulled the car out into the street and started toward our destination the wonderful day I had hoped for. On our festive ride we both talked about everything in our lives and everything else under the sun. She loved football and basketball and that right there was a big plus. Yet, when it came to me speaking up, I guess I would have to say, I lied my ass off about almost everything I was saying. However, I only lied because I didn't want to chase this beautiful lady away. So, I had to paint this almost-perfect picture for her because other than that, she wouldn't have been fucking with no street nigga like me. Nonetheless, we rode laughing and feeling each other to the point it seemed like we been knowing each other for years.

Jasmine had told me that she was from Minnesota and that she had moved to Cleveland because her job at Children's Services had transferred her. She said she was single, which was hard for me to believe. But, I could live with it. She also told me she had no children. That was cool with me because I didn't have any either. Every word that she spoke from her lips, I wanted to catch with my tongue. I swear I did. She was what a nigga needed in his life and I was feeling her big time. I knew she was feeling my style because she kept putting her well-manicured fingers on my thigh every time she laughed.

We had finally arrived at the nice restaurant that I had picked out for this perfect occasion. I hoped it would be satisfying to her. I had picked out a trendy spot called, John Q's Steak House that was located downtown in Public Square. Here a muthafucka got to choose from melt-in-your-mouth, certified, Angus beef, black pepper strip steaks, pork chops, or a twenty-four-ounce Porterhouse. Right here is where you were going to find the best steak dinners the city had to offer.

After a few hours of eating and getting to know each other a bit more, I found myself pulling back up in front of her crib. She told me that she had things to do tonight and had to get ready for work the next morning. So, staying out late wasn't going to happen but, she said, "Anthony, I truly enjoyed myself with you tonight and I apologize that I had to cut things short. Believe you did everything right as a gentleman should have and I would love to go out again. The next date is on me and I'm going to come pick you up."

I said, "Well, I'm glad that you enjoyed yourself and I'll be waiting for that date."

I walked around to the passenger's side of the car to

open her door and in return, she gave me a gentle smile. I then walked her to the front door of her house to let her know at that moment, I was her protector and for that gesture, she gave me a kiss on the cheek.

DAVE:

I was chillin' in the ride, listening to some old Gerald Levert songs that brung back some helluva memories for a nigga. I mean each and every one those love songs used to help a nigga get into some panties. Real talk! Back then a cat didn't have to use his mouth piece. All he had to do was let Gerald get the girl in the mood, then it was on and popping. On some real shit, it was still hard for me to believe that he and his brother were no longer with us, sharing those great love songs with the city and the world. Damn! The city was going to miss both of them.

An hour had skipped past like a young girl playing hop-scotch as I waited for these two niggas to catch up with me on 55th and Broadway. I don't' know what was taking them all day. But, I was tired of watching these two wine heads argue and fight over this one damned bottle of warm cheap wine.

I was almost ready to give up when I had finally spotted them pulling into the parking lot. One was pushing a red and black Can-Am Spyder RJ Roadster with that unique three-wheeled stance, while the other was pushing a yellow and black CBR 1000 RR. Both riders chose not to wear a helmet, ignoring the state rules and regulations. But who, nowadays, followed rules?

"Dee, what up, baby?" Skeet was a high yellow brother

with green eyes and the older of the two niggas staring me down from their bikes like two thirsty hounds. Once upon a time, Skeet had crazy hoop game with a crazy, wicked, jump shot. But, ignoring the skills he was blessed with, this nigga allowed the streets to change the rotation of his game. Now he was plain ole crazy because of the cigarettes he loved to dip into that embalming fluid. That promising career he could've had went down the drain like dirty bath water because he was now addicted to getting it the ski-mask way.

Still straddling the bike, Skeet said, "If you called both of us, then that means we got some heads to bust open like water balloons. And if that's true, then you already know we both down for the cause."

I glanced over at Malik who was nodding his head up and down in agreement, not saying a word. All I had to do was point the lick out to these two hyperactive niggas and it was a done deal. It didn't' matter what the perks was, you just better be on top of your shit because they sure in hell was going to be on theirs.

I reached over and turned my music down a little bit and said, "Yeah, I got a lick for us and I need for ya'll to roll with me."

Malik wasn't as light as his older brother or as tall. However, he was the more treacherous of the two. He played no games when it came to cocking and squeezing those metals. Finally speaking up, Malik said, "You already know we down with you. You keep it real with us and it's never no bullshit when it's time to pay up. Just let us know where and when. You know how to get in touch with us, baby."

Our conversation consisted of just that. After words

was exchanged and everything was in agreement, I called Nikki and told her to be ready because I was on my way to pick her up. I wanted to make sure that I kept my foot on Nikki's ass too. I couldn't afford for anyone to fuck this lick up right here. However, she told me not to bother picking her up because she was being entertained by the fat nigga we was scheming on choking out. So, I told her to hit me up when she was done entertaining his fat ass.

I respected this bitch because she made sure she was all right out in these streets. Nikki took care of her business. She never came to the party with her hands out. She would rather sell some of that sweet pussy before she found herself asking a nigga for anything. Therefore, I found a way for her to keep her dignity and her pussy hole tight all in one and that was by getting her to set these tender dick-ass niggas up. A good fucking or sucking would always open a bunch of these weak niggas up.

It's been like over two years now and we were still rolling tough. Hopefully, this would be our last lick because I was getting to old for this shoot 'em up bang bang shit.

GINA:

I had just gotten off the phone with Jazz. I won't front. I was very excited that she asked me if I wanted to go shopping with her. Did I want to go? Was she serious? Hell to the yeah I wanted to go with her because I was trying to get in close with her. I wanted to rub elbows with the niggas she was dealing with. I bet she messing around with some birdy boys that niggas wasn't hip too. Most likely some out-of-town niggas that didn't have to keep a close eye on her ass. Well, not matter who or what, I know I was going to be a part of it.

I was up in the car with this young nigga off St. Clair. He was out here trying to make a name for himself in the world of hustling. He wanted to be seen as some flashy type with a trophy bitch on his side. That meant he had to pay to play. Ain't shit free no more around here, sugar!

After sucking this young, ugly nigga dry and running some game on his ass about me needing to get home, he finally caught my drift and dropped me off. Standing in the parking lot, gazing at the apartment before entering, I truly hated going in there. I hated stepping my fresh pedicure feet into this place, but my son was in there and that was my life right three. A year ago, I didn't have to worry about all these fiends, crack pipes, and my mother being screwed right in the kitchen in front of anyone who would look. I had my own spot out in Bedford that I loved and kept together. But, when my boyfriend, Zay, dumb-ass, went to jail for drugs again, I had to move. Now I'm stuck here with this bullshit.

I walked into the house that I dreaded and seen Jordan. I rushed to give him a kiss and hug. I missed my little man and it was a blessing to see his handsome face everyday. Glancing to the left of the couch, I saw my mother watching television acting as if I wasn't even there. So, I played the same game and ignored her too, as I ran up the stairs to jump into the shower.

Smelling so fresh and so clean, I called Jazz and told her to come and pick me up in an hour. She agreed. She was a pretty girl and niggas stayed trying to get at her. But, there was something else about her that I couldn't put my well-manicured fingers on. I don't know what it was about her. But, soon, I would figure it out. I was good as hell at figuring shit out that didn't have anything to do with my ass.

After I got dressed, I checked myself out in the mirror. I looked absolutely beautiful. I rushed to cook something for Jordan before I headed out the door. There was no telling when I would be coming back into the house, especially if I found me something real nice that wanted to get a little acquainted with what I had to offer a nigga whose pockets met my satisfaction.

"Mommy, Mommy! Look what Grandma bought for me." After scooping a forkful of mashed potatoes from his plate next to the fried chicken, I took a glance in his direction and seen that he was holding up a fire engine. I couldn't believe what I was seeing. This had to be some type of trick. Mom always spent all her money on booze and booze only. I took a look at my mother. She was looking real gloomy and down. I won't lie. It hurt me to see her like that.

"Ma, thank you so much for buying that toy for Jordan. I truly appreciate it." She nodded her head, peering at me with those depressing eyes. Then, she walked upstairs. I didn't know what the fuck was going on. I really didn't give a damn, to be honest. I told her thank you and I showed her my appreciation. What else did she want me to do?

I finished feeding Jordan, gave him his bath, and placed him in his favorite Sponge Bob pajamas. I grabbed my purse and keys to get ready to leave. Jazz had just called and said she was in the parking lot. I yelled up the stairs to my mother to let her know I was about to go and I pulled out. As I went outside, I looked towards my mother's bedroom window. I could see her sad face pressed tightly to the smudged, glass window. This now began to bother me, but not to the point I would terminate my shopping trip. Fuck dat!

SUKI:

I made my way from the germ-infested motel to the downtown, crowded bus station by taking alleys and catching a taxi with a Nigerian driver who smelled of sweat and beer. Making it downtown was a helluva task because the entire scene I had experienced on these Chicago streets a couple of hours ago was now all over the T.V. and radio stations. The police did not have an accurate sketch of the suspect except that he was a black male who looked very troubled. This was cool with me because there was a bunch of troubled black males in Chicago.

Perched up on one of the benches in the bus terminal waiting for that special someone to pick me up, I sat inspecting the police walking around with their mangy mutts looking at those who looked at them with suspicion in their eyes. Sitting next to me was some old white lady pretending to read a magazine while taking odd looks at me as if I wanted to stick her up or some shit. If the old lady had any clue that I was on some other shit right now, then maybe she wouldn't have moved her purse to the other side of her body.

Ignoring the old hag, I, too, picked up something to read 'til that someone came to pick me up. After an hour or so, I peeked around the two-day-old Chicago Tribune to see someone I recognized. Janaia's sexy ass was coming through the swinging doors. She looked as if she was in town to handle business. I loved her style because she was about her business.

Damn! I was happy to see her. I swear I could've cried like a damned baby.

Scraping over the terminal, Janaia finally saw me standing up looking dead at her. Making her way towards me, she said, "Suki, you alright?" I could tell that she was really concerned about my well-being and all. But, I didn't have no time for these sentimental moments she was trying to share with the kid. I was on the run from some ill shit and we both needed to get the fuck out Chicago as quickly as possible.

"Yeah, I'm cool, baby," I told her. "But we really need to be getting on the road." Janaia at me as if she was trying to figure me out like a riddle. She finally turned around and started walking towards the exit doors. As we got our stroll on towards the exit doors, I noticed two redneck cops walking towards us at a speedy pace. Oh shit! Did these pigs know something I didn't know? If so, I had to make up my mind to either die for this damned paper or go do life in prison for murder. "Fuck dat," I muttered.

I positioned my hand in the waistband of my True Religion jeans and decided to cowboy style this one out. I ain't gon' front. I was scared to death. I didn't want to die in no Chicago bus terminal with two bags of unspent money. I wanted to get a chance to spend at least a dollar of this shit.

The closer the police got to me, the more my hand squeezed tighter around the butt of the .44 ready to take the top off one of these cock suckers. Blood was going to be painted all over this bitch. I wasn't going to be the only one to hit up, baby. When I thought all hell was about to be unleashed, the two police officers sped right pass me and Janaia towards some young, Hispanic kid who was arguing with another officer at the other end of the terminal.

Oh shit! I had to let out the air that I had trapped in my lungs. I almost shit myself for the second time today. I couldn't wait 'til we made it out of the state of Illinois.

Finally reaching the scanless city of Cleveland without a problem, I expressed my thanks to Janaia as she dropped me off in front of my apartment. I had offered the nosey bitch a couple of bucks for her time. But, she refused to take the small change I was trying to toss her way. I wasn't trying to kick it with her like that anyways, so I didn't give two fucks if she didn't want to take the money.

Before pulling off, Janaia shouted, "What you want me to tell Hectic?"

I didn't want her to tell that nigga shit, to be honest. Damn! Did she think I was supposed to report back to this nigga or something?

"I don't want you to tell that nigga nothing. I made it back and that's that. What else is there to say?" I could tell by the way Janaia twisted up her face that I had hit a nerve with her. I knew Hectic was her man and I knew she was going to tell him what I said. And to be truthful, I didn't care one bit about it. I'm rich, bitch!

DAVE:

I was stuck at a red light on 140th and St. Clair when I looked over at the gas station and seen a familiar face. It was a face that needed to be talked to and that's what I was going to do.

The kid was leaning on a blue and black mountain bike

running his gums off to some pretty, young thang that was thicker than two Snicker bars put together. She had her hair all popped. I loved a girl that kept her nails and toes fly. She was rocking a tight white T-shirt and some tight blue jean shorts that defined her butt cheeks and a tattoo that said, "Goodies." Instead of watching this kid and trying to decide on what to do, I noticed how the young girl didn't want to be bothered by this cornball-ass nigga. She kept trying to walk away from his weak conversation. "Fuck it," I said to myself. I pulled the car into the gas station.

Pulling close to them both, I rolled down the passenger's window and gave Pete a small call, "Homeboy." The way the young girl's face twisted up like corn rows in nappy young nigga's head, you would've thought Pete stupid ass would've got the message that something, in fact, was wrong. Not paying close attention to life's inborn survival skills, this nigga turned around to face the barrel of my Mac-11 cocked and ready to explode him all over the hot pavement and gas pumps.

"Go ahead and try to run, nigga," I warned him. "I bet yo dumb ass don't get far." Pete had no idea what was going on and I knew the nigga had thoughts about taking his chances on booking it down the block. But I also knew he thought about the hot slugs he couldn't outrun.

So, he threw his hands up in the air and said, "You can have it all, baby." He started reaching inside his pockets as I stopped him quickly, "I don't want your money and get your muthafuckin' hands out your pockets. I want you to get in the car. That's what I want. Not now, but right now. And I ain't playing no games with your ass."

Glancing back at the young girl who now had a smirk on

her pretty face, Pete got off the bike allowing it to slam hard to the ground and jumped unwillingly inside the air-conditioned car. You could never leave a witness to a murder because, at any given time, the police could come kicking in your door because some ho-ass nigga snitched you out.

HECTIC:

I had a magnificent day with Jasmine. She was the first woman that had me feeling the way that I was feeling and shit. She had a nigga feeling all mushy like a nigga used to feel back in elementary school when a young playa was trying to holla at the cutie on the swings. Jasmine had me feeling different. It was bugging me out because I couldn't get my mind off her sexy ass.

My phone rang and I seen it was Dave. He wanted to meet him at this garage out in Collinwood—the place we both kept hidden from everyone in the crew. We had rented the garage to do our personal business at, plus to have a place to lay low where no one would know how to reach either one of us.

Making it to the garage in no time, I spotted Dave's Ford Fusion and pulled up next to it. As I strolled into the small garage to see what was going on, I could hear Beanie Sigel rhyming in the background spitting that mad flow.

We had a couple of motorcycles up in here, a few leather chairs, a leather couch, a forty-seven-inch flat screen to play games on, and an old '87 Cadillac standing on three wheels. It was real nice and comfortable set up to chill in, expect it did smell like gasoline and old car oil.

What Dave wanted to chatter to me about was finally exposed to me when I seen this lame Pete tied up to a wooden chair. His hands were taped to the arms of the chair. His feet were tied up tight with some ropes Dave must've found around the garage. Pete's mouth had grey duct tape running across it to prevent him from making unnecessary crying out to the public. Checking out the scenery, I also noticed plastic covering the floor and walls that encircled the nigga. I couldn't figure out why. I still hadn't located Dave so I took it he was still in the back.

As a result of not seeing Dave, I marched towards Pete. He had tears rolling down his face and he had pissed on himself earlier in the day because the front of his jean shorts was soaking wet.

"Well, well, well," I said. "Look what we got here. I thought you would've skipped town, knowing I was looking for your ass. But I guess I was wrong. Damn! You in a fucked up position now, ain't you?"

Hearing someone behind me, I spun around to see Dave wearing a white apron. "I told you I had something for you," he said. "Now it's time to take out the trash."

I gave Dave a moderate smile and cruised over to the old Caddie that should've been fixed a long time ago. I cracked open the trunk and pulled out the sniper's rifle we had stashed. Dave yelled loudly over the music, "Naw! Put that shit back. We ain't gon' need that. I got something real special for this nigga. Hold up for a second." Dave walked away laughing, while I put the rifle back in the trunk of the ride. When I closed the trunk and seen what Dave had in his hands, I just stood there.

Dave was standing in the doorway with a chainsaw

hanging from his hands. The expression on his face said there was no turning back.

"Hold up, Dave," I said. "What's up with you?"

Dave walked over towards Pete and said, "What you mean what's up with me? I'm about to take care of this problem you let run around the streets for weeks. You and that nigga Cool let this nigga run around the city after witnessing you blow holes in his boy. We can't afford for these types to run the streets freely. Are you crazy?" He didn't allow me to get a word in that we had been looking for this nigga, Dave reached for the cord and gave the handy machine two sharp pulls before it came to life with a large whine.

Sensing the move that was about to go down, Pete started bouncing around in his chair as if he would shoot straight out the roof if he bounced hard enough. "Sit back and learn something, homie." Dave grabbed the remote to the Alpine system and revved it up some more. Then he walked up to the bouncing Pete and, without hesitation, hit the nigga right in the shoulder with the heavy machine. Within seconds, blood leaped from under the chainsaw as it continued ripping right through Pete like the teeth of a Great White shark on a baby seal's ass. The pain was so unbearable that Pete passed out before his arm had fallen to the side of the chair.

Satisfied with his work, Dave then went to the other shoulder and did the same thing. Blood shot over the walls covered with plastic. The place looked as if a child had been finger painting a picture for a school project.

Looking at both arms dangling from the side of the chair and the blood gushing out the open holes was gross and forced me to look away. This whole scene looked like something from a horror flick as tendons and veins hung like strings with no puppets attached to them.

Dave then walked to the Pete's side and placed the heavy machine up to his throat. The sharp metal teeth gripped his skin tightly and started chopping and twisting the flesh that covered his esophagus. You could hear the chainsaw ripping and clawing at the thin bones as it bit hard and rough through Pete's limp body. Within seconds, Pete's head tumbled to the floor like a heavy bowling ball.

I had to spin to the side and throw up the little food I had in my stomach. It wasn't everyday that a nigga got to see a person get chain sawed to death. Feel me?

After wiping my mouth clean, I looked up to see Pete's body jerking from left to right as Dave was cutting through this nigga's midsection. When the hungry blades finally touched his spine, you could hear the hard metal teeth grinding up against the bone that kept his body attached. After Dave got finished with his small project, he turned the chainsaw off and kicked Pete's torso to the floor letting all his insides slide out to the plastic. Ewww!

There lay Pete in pieces like Humpty Dumpty. Dave turned around, looking at me and said, "It's done, baby. Come on, let's clean this shit up before it start stinking up in this bitch. Grab those four plastic bags off the couch and hurry up, nigga."

We bagged up the body parts and placed them all in separate bags and tossed the shit in the backseat of the Caddie. We then sponged down the walls and floors where the business went down at and made sure we left no proof to the naked eye. Then we each grabbed the water hose and washed our bodies down with water to let the leftover blood wash down the drain. We both took off our clothes and placed those shits into another plastic bag and tossed that shit in the back of the Caddie as well. No evidence, no case.

CHAPTER 5

JASMINE:

As I pulled into the parking lot of the King Kennedy Projects, I noticed a few groups of men standing around wearing mean mugs like a pair of old jeans. I decided to give Gina a call and let her know I was downstairs waiting for her. I didn't want to get out of the car and be bothered by all the madness I felt was hanging in the parking lot like a wrinkled shirt.

Leaning back in my seat listening to the oldies but goodies station waiting for Gina to bring her ass on, I observed some little children running around having a blast tossing water balloons at each other. Their mothers or whoever they were, were right there with them talking shit, blowing weed, and sipping cans of beer. However, the small children and women wasn't what caught my eye. What caught my eye was the young niggas that sat in the dark behind trees like wolves ready to attack a wounded prey.

I had seen the four hoodlums sneaking behind me from the back of my car. So, I sneaked out my .9mm and placed it between my legs and waited. My car windows were already rolled down because of the heat and I guess the young males took it as an open invitation to pull up on me. "Hey, pretty. What you looking for?" I didn't know which kid said it, but I had become aware of one kid vigorously pushing his hand into my window. He was holding a pile of rocks.

"What you need?" The other three then tried to squeeze into the picture to show me what they had to offer.

"Look, I'm not here to buy no damned drugs. Get your damned hands out my car," I told them.

Some young kid with a mouth full of gold teeth said, "Bitch, what you sitting right here for then? You the police or something?"

Ewww! I wanted to jump out of the car and bend that little boy right over my knee and spank his ass for having such a nasty mouth.

However, my thoughts were interrupted by someone screaming. "Tuffy, if you don't get away from that damned car, I'm going to tell your father on your ass." Gina was rushing towards the car looking like one of the dancers from the old television show "In Living Colors." Her hair was three different colors. She wore earrings big enough for a dog to jump through, and she had her ass hanging out of these super tight shorts.

I wanted to laugh at this damned girl. But, I changed my mind because I didn't want to cause any problems between us at this moment. I needed to get this information from her man-crazed ass.

"Get the hell away from the car, boy." Gina was

swinging her big Gucci purse in the direction of the young thug wannabe. She damned near knocked him and everyone else in her way over. Gina jumped into the car smelling like a gallon of perfume. She left glitter over everything she touched. Sucking her white teeth, she said, "Girl, I'm sorry about that. But, these the projects and you know how that shit goes."

I wanted to tell her, "No. I don't know how it goes." But, instead, I backed the car out and said, "Damn! Girl we ain't going nowhere but to the mall."

Gina who now had a sucker in her mouth, replied, batting her fake eyelids, "Shit! Ain't no telling who I might see, girl."

Me and Gina had been out a couple of times. I kept at her about her relationship with Marcus. I already knew her boyfriend was a part of his crew. So, I knew she had some way of introducing me to the fat man.

One day while we were having lunch up in Beachwood, I said, "When you going to take me to meet that cat, Marcus?" Gina was about to bite into her sandwich. She stopped in mid-bite and said, "Girl, he got a swimming pool party tomorrow night and I meant to tell you that. Damn! We can go up there tomorrow night if that's cool with you."

I couldn't believe that it was that easy and I was happy that I didn't have to work hard to meet this nigga. "No, it's not going to be no problem. We have ourselves another date, girl." I was finally going to meet the fat man.

SUKI:

I scurried into the bedroom and tossed both the bags

on my bed. I looked quickly around the room as if seeing it for the first time. Then, I had pulled out the .44 to validate that no one was laying on me inside my own apartment. I ain't felt safe for over a day. Before I sat back and counted up all the dead presidents, I was going to make sure that I was out of harm's way.

After I paced quietly around the small apartment, making sure that I checked every room, I began to relax, knowing I was alone. Seeing there was no nigga trying to play peek-a-boo with a nigga, I made my way back to the bedroom. I tossed the gun on the bed and, clutching the earliest bag, I dispensed its stuffing. I watched closely as the dead presidents floated out of the bag like autumn leaves. I then snatched up the second bag and watched in disbelief as green cash over flowed my bad like foam from a root beer soda. There was a mound of cash on the bed and a few bills scattered on the floor. I stood in place, fascinated by the splendor of the mighty green.

All that rigid grinding and head busting was over with for the kid. The corrupt and foul life I was living had finally paid off for me. It was now time to jump out the Range truck on these broke niggas. Hectic and the rest of those lames could kiss my ashy ass because it was all about me now. Niggas out on the streets were splattering each other's brains over slabs of concrete and grinding dumb hard for the status that I'm at right now. The sweet status of stability!

I'm sick and tired of running behind other niggas like I'm some type of groupie. I made my bones out in those wild streets and I was tired of Hectic this, Hectic that. Fuck that shit, man. It's about Suki and that's the only thing that I was concerned with now. Straight up!

I sat stacking every thousand I counted, and then I placed them into stacks of tens and came up with $385,400. I chuckled out loud so hard that I fell off the bed. Hitting my head hard on floor. I ignored the small sting I was now feeling. I was too happy to think about the pain I had just suffered. I was about to come down and watch these niggas' faces turn colors like a new paint job.

First I had to put some of this money up and go call this white bitch that would freak with a nigga if the paper was right. Well, I guess there was about to be a lot of freaking going on because my money was all the way right.

HECTIC:

I was awakened by a lot of clatter. It seemed like shit was bouncing off the walls all around me. Now that I was wide awake, I couldn't do nothing but pay attention to the screaming and crying coming from next door where this young pair went through it like every other damned day. I don't know if this was a method that these white muthafuckas used to show their love and dedication towards each other, but the whole thing was getting on my damned nerves.

Continuing to take notice of the plates and other flying object crashing against my wall, I rolled over so see how early in the morning it was. After distinguishing the crimson red numbers that screamed 8:15am, I knew it was time to get my ass up. However, I was still tired from last night's event. And I'm not talking about from all the shots of Remy I was tossing back or the chainsaw massacre Dave put down either. I was talking about the experience I had with these two damned girls that was lying in the bed with me at this moment.

Glancing to my left, I watched the two silhouette female bodies sleeping peacefully up under my grey silk sheets. Yet, both of these bitches needed to get up out of my spot for the reason being this wasn't any damned Motel 6. Rolling up out of the bed and walking to the end of the king-sized bed, I politely, and I mean, politely snatched the silk sheets off the two sleeping, naked women. "Yo! It's time to get the fuck up," I shouted.

"Damn, Hec! Why you tripping and shit?" the black thick girl said. Her name was Veronica and she had the biggest tits I've ever seen in my life. She tried to reach for the sheets behind her head, and take it like a fuckin' Gangster. She sat on her elbows just looking at me.

"Did ya'll even hear what I just said?" I asked. "Ya'll gots to get the hell up out of here. This ain't no damned sleepover. Now get the fuck up, get dressed, and bounce." I grabbed my cell phone and marched my ass to the bathroom connected to my bedroom and sat right on the toilet.

Keeping my eyes on both these ho's, I dialed up Cool's number because I ain't heard from the nigga in a couple of days. Hearing the voicemail pick up once again, I then called Janaia who told me she had picked Suki up. But when she told me that the nigga was acting real strange, I knew something was up with him. But, that was Suki and if a nigga knew Suki, then he knew he stayed in the mix of some trouble.

I told Janaia not to worry her head about it and to come over and pick up this money. Baby girl wasn't pressed for the money because she said, "Real muthafuckas did real shit," and hung up on me. That's why I had her on my team.

I was about to hit up Jasmine but then changed my

mind because I didn't want her to hear me kicking these dumb bitches out my apartment. I grimaced once or twice, and then allowed for my load to splash in the toilet water while the two girls looked at me madly. "Papi, you a straight up mess. You know that? How you going to treat us like we some damned streetwalkers?"

Placing my phone on the sink and reaching for the toilet paper to wipe my ass, I said, "Yeah, whatever you say. This is my damned house and I do what the hell I want to do. Now get the fuck out." After wiping my ass and flushing the toilet, I jumped up to escort both bitches out my establishment.

"You ain't shit, Hectic. For real." Veronica said while sullenly stepping out into the hallway.

"Well, sometimes that's the way it goes," I told her and slammed the door on both of them.

On my way to get into the shower, I grabbed the phone off the sink and decided to make one more call. I needed to see what was going on with Suki. Plus, I needed to tell him about the lick we had set up. When he picked up, I said, "Wazzup, nigga."

Suki replied, "Hec, what's the deal with you?"

I said, "Damn! What's going on with you? I ain't heard from you since you got back from the Chi."

Suki didn't say nothing for a couple of seconds, then said, "What the fuck you talking about, nigga? You act like you my Pops or something. Yo! You gots to chill with that shit, man."

I was shocked by what I was hearing. Puzzled and stunned, I said, "Hold up, nigga. I don't know who you think you talking to, but you need to change your tone, nigga."

After another short pause, Suki said, "Check this out, Hec. Fuck you, nigga. I got my own shit going on and I don't owe you any explanation, so with that I'm out."

I stood in the middle of my bathroom butt naked, goose bumps rushing all over my chilled body as a dial tone buzzed loudly in my ear. This bitch ass nigga had hung up on me! I couldn't believe it.

Where did all this come from and what the fuck happened up in Chicago? I knew he did something. I just couldn't put my finger on it yet. But if this is how he wanted to play his hand, then two could play the same game.

SHANTEL:

I was fuming with Hectic. To make matters even worse, I was in love with this punk ass nigga. But I was also sick and tired of him just doing me wrong. I had promised myself a long time ago to get the next nigga who tried to play me out. I knew Hectic was street and carried the credentials of being a hardcore thug nigga. But, at this instant, I had to play thug too. If he wanted to play games, then games we shall play. I wasn't going to let him get away without a fight. I was willing to go the full rounds with him toe to muthafuckin' toe.

Sitting on my comfortable, queen-sized bed watching, basketball "Housewives", and sipping on a Virgin Daiquiri, I kept looking at the safe that sat in the corner of my bedroom. Feeling a little tipsy from the alcohol I had consumed, I got up and stumbled over to the safe. After a few turns and a few clicks, I popped the safe open, reached inside and grabbed the chrome long barrel .357 pistol I kept with me for protection.

I couldn't do nothing but gaze at the heavy chunky pistol for a few moments. Yeah! We'll see who'll get the last laugh on this one, I thought.

Dressed in a silk robe that clung to my hips tightly like a wig on a baldhead bitches head, I staggered over to the phone and pushed seven numbers that I knew backwards and frontwards. When no one picked up, I decided to leave a small message.

"Baby, I'm sorry for all that I said. I love you and miss you very much and I need you with me. I got something over here for you and I wish you would come over and get it, baby. And I promise, after this, I won't bother you again. Please call me." I then blew a wet kiss into the phone before hanging it up. Yeah, I'm going to kill your black ass and that way ain't no bitch gone be able to fuck with your sorry ass again, I thought.

Jumping back on the bed and taking another sip of my drink, I then started to put bullets in the gun reciting, "He loves me. He loves me not."

CHAPTER 6

HECTIC:

Before my day could begin the way that I required, I needed to make sure that Cool was doing okay. I ain't heard one word from him since that night we treated his ass to a few strippers who did whatever we asked for as long as we made it rain. I hope he wasn't on no fuck shit like that nigga Suki bitch-ass was on earlier. I understood that Cool had just got out of the joint and a nigga wanted to lay up with some pussy. But, damn!

Pulling up to the little complex out in Maple Heights where Cool's scanless girl resided, I peeped Cool's red Chevy SS in the parking lot hidden behind a tore-up Suburban that had seen some better days. That right there was a high-quality sign that he was chillin' and getting those eighteen months of frustration out his system. But, something deep inside me told me to go check up on my boy.

See, the little skeezer Cool was laid up with was kinda holding him down by putting a few bucks on his books, sending him a few food boxes, and visiting him like a real woman was supposed to do for a real nigga while doing his bid. But word on the streets was that this skeezer was tipping out on my boy with some Jamaican cat. Yeah, some islander that was supposed to be pushing heavy pounds of Kush around the city. How true it was, I don't know. But when the story involved one of my boys, then I had to see what was what.

I got to the door and frivolously knocked on it a few times, trying not to be too noisy. Getting no response, I knocked a little louder and called out his name. Still no answer. I looked up and down the hallways to see if anyone was watching me. Then, I grabbed the door knob and gave it a small twist. The wooden door gave way for me to walk right in. Once inside, I was greeted by total darkness. The drapes were drawn tight like some shoe strings in a pair of old worn down Timberlands. On top of that, it was hot as hell in the small apartment. "Cool, where you at?" I called out, reaching around in the darkness to find the light switch to see where I was going. I tripped over something, almost falling over it. Flicking the light on, I discovered I had tripped over one of the sofa cushions. From the disarray of the apartment, I could tell that someone ran up in this bitch looking for something or someone. Not feeling trouble-free about my findings, this whole situation in front of me forced me to grab my pistol.

Walking carefully around the house, trying not to be heard, I noticed no one was in the dining-room or small laundry room that sat off the kitchen. Swiftly, I made my way down the hallway towards the first bedroom. I opened the door slowly and seen this was where the eight-year-old girl slept. Nothing seemed to be disturbed and all her stuffed animals and toys were intact.

Moving on to the second bedroom, I gave the knob a small turn to let myself in. Once the door was ajar, I took a few steps in. Welcoming me at the door like a girl scout selling those mint cookies, was a smell that hit me like a leaping left hook from Mike Tyson. Damn! That smell told me someone was lying stiff as a surfboard a few feet from me.

The strong stench that had been trapped in the room for days made me gag. I turned the light on. My boy was stretched out across the bed with half his head missing. One half was still attached to his skeleton, while the other half lay up against the wooden bedpost. The only noise was the rapid hard thuds of my heart beat and the flies that circled the corpse like famished vultures at meal time.

GINA:

I staggered into the apartment like a drunk reeling out of his favorite bar after downing too many shots of Jim Bean. The apartment was quiet as a mouse. Everyone was asleep. It was three in the damned morning. My mother was stretched out on one end of the couch with her mouth wide open like a dark deep cave. My son was curled up on the other end of the couch sleeping peacefully. I wanted to pick my little man up and put him in his own bed, but I chose not to because I wasn't sure if I could carry myself one more step.

I tiptoed across the room, trying my hardest not to knock anything over. I staggered over Jordan's fire engine almost breaking my ankle in these damned high heeled pumps. Grabbing the wall with one hand and balancing myself with the other one stopped me from falling into the glass coffee table and breaking my damned neck. If this nigga that I was out with tonight had drunk more of the bottle with me, then maybe I wouldn't be this damned geeked and tripping over shit.

Clenching my teeth and sucking up the pain from the light twist to my ankle, I finally made it to the stairs and gave them a small climb to my bedroom. Shutting the door lightly, I threw down my purse flopped my ass on the cool bed, and stared at the off- white ceiling. It wouldn't stop spinning if I had paid it to. I couldn't believe that I was s living out of the same room that I had grown up in. This was the same room that I had sneaked that boy Smoke into to play grown up when I was thirteen. Shit! I still had Li'l Kim, Biggie Small, Tyrese, and Bone Thug & Harmony posters glued to my damned walls—as if I were still in high school. I couldn't believe where my life was now. To be honest, I had no idea where it was going to take me.

Zay was back in jail because he couldn't stop catching drug charges and once again, I was left out here to fend for me and Jordan. I had no education, no job, and the only talent I had down pat was tricking these soft-ass niggas out of their shit. I'm not going to lie. I did enjoy all the attention that I got from these cats, whether it was positive or negative. Long as I was getting some money out of it, it didn't matter to me one bit. Men were going to notice me and that was all that counted.

I had talked to Marcus' fat ass and told him about my girl Jazz who always be asking about him. I couldn't figure out why the bitch was so up beat on his beefy ass. I knew everyone in the city knew who Marcus was. But, she sure in the hell was going extra hard to meet him. Maybe she had a nose like me and could smell the money dripping off his fat, turkey-and-gravy-smelling ass. Maybe she was trying to set herself up something nice like I tried to do when I first approached him. On the real shit, I wasn't even trying to kick it was Zay's skinny ass. I was trying to lay that fat nigga down. He was the one will all the money and benefits for a bitch like me. But things didn't turn out the way that I had wished for them to go. So I had to take what I could get.

I rose off the bed to take off my clothes so I could wash up before sliding into my warm bed. On my small trip, I noticed my mother heading into her bedroom. It had been some time since I looked into her old face to recognize the pain in her eyes. Maybe it was me just being selfish because I didn't want her to see the pain in mine.

"Mom, what's wrong with you?" I asked her. You've been walking around here all week like this."
Putting her head down as if she was ashamed of life, she spun around to face me and said, "Gina, I went to see the doctor last week and I found out that…" A tear came crawling out the corner of her eye as she continued, "I have breast cancer and I'm scared to death. I fucked up my whole life and now there is no chance for me to make things better."

I won't lie. I had to take a step back because I was traumatized by what I had just heard. I didn't agree with a lot of shit my mother did. And, I'm pretty sure she didn't agree with a lot of shit I did. But, I would never wish death on her. Never that!

I was fucked up by what she had just told me. What was I to say? We ain't had no serious talks with each other in years.

She ain't never told me about no birds and bees or about these nothing-ass niggas that would trick a bitch into the bed.

What was I supposed to do? Maybe I should just walk right past her like she used to do to me so many nights when I was young and needed her. Or maybe I should act concerned, give her a hug, and keep it moving. In no way did we share a tight bond like a daughter and mother should have. But still, I had to be there for her no matter what type of problems we had with each other. She was my mother and that remained a fact. I walked over to my mother who felt frail in my arms and said, "Mom, we can beat this together. I really don't know what to do or say that will make things better. But, whatever it is, I'm going to be there for you." She buried her face against my left tit and cried. This brought tears to my eyes. We stood holding each other.

The next morning, I woke up to the smell of breakfast floating around the house like Casper the Friendly Ghost. I mean, I ain't smelled no breakfast in this house since the last time I cooked it and that shit was a long damned time ago. I had to be dreaming or I had to be hungrier than a muthafucka because I knew my nose wasn't playing no tricks with my growling stomach.

Rushing to investigate this strange sensation, I wiped the sleep from my eyes, grabbed my robe, and made my way down the stairs. First look into the living-room, I seen my son watching his cartoons. He said, "Look ma! I got panny cakes and juice."

He sure in the hell did! I told him, "I see, baby. It looks good too." I walked over to Jordan, kissed him on his forehead, and then walked into the kitchen where my mother was cooking all types of dishes like she was participating in some cooking contest. She turned around and gave me a smile and asked was I hungry. I was too shocked to give her the answer that she was in search of.

"Girl, you better get you a plate of this food. I ain't cook all this shit for you to sit and look at it. Now get a plate, girl." She had made pancakes, cheesed eggs, sausage links, bacon, and grits and the shit looked hella good. My mother then said, "Gina, I been fucking up and I want to make things better between us. I'm going to leave that drinking and running around with these damned fiends alone. All I got is you and my grandbaby in my life and with the little time that I got left, I want to make it up to you both." I couldn't hold back the tears.

I walked over and gave her a hug and said, "Mom, you'll be fine and we going to make it past this breast cancer. We'll fight it together. I promise."

HECTIC:

A couple of weeks had flown past like a flock of geese headed south to get away from the cold Cleveland winter. In those two rapid weeks, me and Dave had been scampering around the city looking for Cool's girl and that Rasta nigga she been holed up under. There was nowhere in the city that the bitch or that Island-ass nigga could hide that we wouldn't be able to locate them. I was going to find them muthafuckas no matter what and when I did. I was going to play the judge, prosecutor, and executioner all in one once that opportunity presented itself. In the process of all this madness dealing with this search, today was the day that I had to attend the funeral of my best friend.

Me and Dave had paid for the arrangements for the funeral as well as for the gold casket that my childhood friend was lying in.

It was still tough for me to believe that my nigga was gone and that he would never be coming back. One thing that I had grasped and understood while growing up in this filthy world was that we were all promised to leave this cruel and uncanny world and to never come back.

After everyone had came through the church doors paying their respect to Cool's mother and family for their tragic lost, the chubby preacher with his hair slicked back walked to the pulpit to prepare for his sermon from the good book he held tightly in his obese hands. The sharply-dressed preacher who rocked a gold tooth in his mouth, wore two tight thin chains around his thick neck, and drove a black 2005 Cadillac DTS. He loved the packed church and couldn't wait for the collection basket to be passed around. To him it was all about the Benjamin's., baby, and that thick young seventeen-year-old girl he had been sneaking around with.

Not sure where he wanted to do his business, the preacher then walked from behind the pulpit and was now making his way down to the floor where everyone was seated. He glanced down at his Bible and asked for an, "Amen." The church together mumbled what he was expecting to hear as he walked back and stood in front of the gold casket holding Cool's lifeless body. Looking back into his Bible to make sure that he had his verses right. He was stopped frozen when the front doors of the church opened. Unbending like the Great Wall of China, the fat preacher looked as if he was witnessing

Jesus and his twelve Disciples walking down the aisle towards him.

Noticing everyone staring, I too turned around to witness who had entered. My mouth dropped to the ground like a rotten apple from its tree. Suki punk-ass was strolling down the aisle with three gorgeous girls sashaying behind him carrying bouquets of beautiful flowers and wreaths. Suki was dressed in a razor-sharp, sky blue suit with a yellow silk shirt and some sky blue gators to match his outfit. This nigga ain't never dressed like this before. The last time I seen him in a suit was when we was about thirteen, going to church for Easter with his grandmother.

I ain't seen this cat in weeks and it took for us to have to bury our boy to catch a glimpse of this sucka? The way he was dressing and acting only tells me that Suki had hit a serious lick up in Chicago—or the nigga hit the lottery and he didn't want us to be a part of his winnings. Now shit was adding up and I guess that's why he said we needed to go our separate ways when I talked to him on the phone…Bitch ass nigga!

Suki and the three beautiful girls who followed close behind him, walked up to the casket placing the expensive flowers and wreaths down in front of it. The three stunning girls stood to the side like Deal or No Deal models. Suki then looked inside the coffin at Cool and held a brief conversation with him that only he and Cool could hear. After a few minutes, he then turned around to look for Cool's mother in the crowded church. Once locating her, he made his way over to her with his arms out wide for her to fall deep into like a tub full of warm water and bubbles. While holding her tightly, this no-ass nigga gave me a wink and a hard stare that whispered more than words could ever clarify.

Suki then released his tight grip and reached inside his pockets to share with the world how big his knot of money was. Peeling bills back like a nigga would do a ripened banana, he then gives Cool's mother a nice piece of it while steadily staring me down. So, I took it so say something to him with this meaty .357 I carried up inside the church.

Okay, I was wrong for bringing the hammer up in the house of the Lord. But you never knew when a nigga was going to try some sinful shit and right now was the time to do some crucifying up in this house of the Lord.

I stood up quickly reaching for the .357. Then, I felt Dave grab my hand and say, "Chill my nigga. His time is going to come. But, right now it's about Cool and his family." Dave was right. Cool was about my best friend and today was all about seeing him off to a better place than this raggedy muthafucka we was living in.

Nevertheless, Suki got a chance to realize what was about to transpire and that it was on 'til the break of dawn. If he wanted to play crazy, then I was going to play right along with him. He had me fucked up.

JASMINE:

OMG! I finally got a chance to meet Antonio Marcus and he did seem to have things locked down. He was living up in Shaker Heights, Ohio where a lot of remarkable homes were located. You had to pride yourself on a nice quantity of money to be living up here—especially on the street where he resided.

Before I arrived at the party, Gina had told me while

putting more make-up on her face, "Girl, there gon' be other ballers crawling around the party like insects and you shouldn't spend all your precious energy focusing on Marcus' fat ass."

I truly don't know what her problem was now that we were getting closer to his house. But it seemed she had a bit of an attitude going on. I guess this bitch thought I wanted this fat muthafucka or something. I didn't want his ass. But, I take it Gina's jealousy was popping up and showing its ugly pimpled face. I paid her childish ways no mind because I had bigger fish to fry. Shit! I just hoped I could get Marcus' attention without letting him put his malevolent hands all over me. Ewww!

When Gina and I arrived at the pool party, a crowd of thirsty-ass bitches were permitting men to toss money at them as they took off their garments to the rhymes of Gucci Mane. It killed me to observe these beautiful, young, black women doing any and everything to be up in one these drug pushing nigga's faces. I couldn't understand how a woman would disgrace herself. It was sickening to watch what some of them would do just to get recognized by a bunch of nobodies who, in two or three years, would be doing time in prison.

Me and Gina both walked toward the pool area where everyone was located, looking just as good as the rest of the bitches flaunting themselves around. However, I made sure I wore a sheer around my waist not to show more than I really wanted, yet still just enough to be noticed by the guys. On the other hand, Gina was letting it all hang out. When I say, "Hang out", I mean exactly that! Every step she took, her ass would jiggle like a bowl of cherry Jell-o in a happy child's hands. She was smiling and talking to every damned person we walked by as if she was the 'First Lady' or something.

"Come on, girl. There that nigga is right there," screamed Gina. I looked in the direction that Gina had pointed out and I s couldn't see him. A lot of niggas and females had Marcus surrounded like he was a famous rapper or an up-and-coming movie star.

I almost came up out of my Jimmy Choo sandals trying to keep up with Gina as she rushed over to Marcus. Finally arriving where Marcus was, Gina had to push her way past everyone as if Marcus had been waiting on her his entire life.

"Hey, baby", Gina went rushing to him giving him a big hug and kiss on his fat black cheek as if he was her man. I had finally gotten the chance to get next to the man I was hoping to take down and I have to say, he was one of the ugliest niggas I've ever seen in my entire thirty-three years on this earth. This nigga had a pair of bitty eyes and it looked like he had some type of skin condition that needed to be gazed at by a dermatologist, quickly, before it broke out over his whole body. He had patches in his hair similar to ringworm and he had to have at least three chins. He seemed to weigh about three thirty give or take. Fuck! The whole look was even more gross because of the red Speedo he wore. OMG once again!

Marcus had five gorgeous girls around him when we pulled up. Once he seen us, well, me rather, he said to the five, "Ya'll bitches go find something to do. I got some serious business to take care of." As he said that, he was looking me up and down like I was a piece of fried chicken with extra hot sauce. I felt so damned violated that I wanted to turn around and leave before something foul slipped out my mouth. But, I knew I had a job to do and I had to see this shit through.

Gina's jealous ass had peeped game. She instantly jumped

in swinging her fat ass in his face. "Hey, big daddy. How you doing with your fine self?" Gina tried to sit on his lap but he pushed her to the side to get a better glimpse of me. "And this must be the fabulous Jazz you was telling me about. Damn! You fine, baby."

I hated to do this, but I gave the 'Hungry Hippo' a radiant smile and small blush—just to play my part. I could tell that Gina was furious with me because she gave me a snarling look before walking away.

As I went to call for her, Marcus' fat hand grabbed me around my wrist. "Fuck that bitch!" he said. "We don't need her to have a good time. All we need is your sexy self, these two cold bottles here and of course me. Come on, we can go over in that corner. Get a little acquainted. Feel what I'm saying?"

As much as I wanted to say, "No, I wasn't feeling what he was saying", instead I said, "Sure. Let's do that." Agreeing with the answer I gave him, he hurriedly grabbed my hand and the two bottles of champagne. We both strolled to the secluded area of the party he pointed out.

Having money was really a trip because if any of these bitches would've seen me walking around with this fat, ugly, nasty, sweet-potato-pie-smelling-ass nigga, they would be laughing their pretty little heads off. But since he was caking and had that butter, these bitches were jealous. If jealousy came with a knife; I would've been a stabbed-up bitch.

Marcus poured us a drink and began to talk all this Casanova junk to me about how much I reminded him of his mother and how he was thinking about having a family and he could see me in his future. He also told me he could do things for me that no other man could do and that wasn't even including the taking care of me part. I swear I wanted to laugh at this fool. But, the more he kept talking, the more information his dumb ass was giving me. He was telling me how much dope he was supplying the city, where he was getting his drugs from, and what his next plans was going to be. I had all this shit recorded with the small instrument I had in my purse. He even pointed out the Detroit boys Petro told me he was supposed to be doing business with. I guess his informant was on top of his snitching ways.

As he continued to talk and I continued to push his hands away from me, I was looking for Gina because I had enough information on him. I was beginning to fall asleep listening to all this jibber jabber. "No, I ain't never been to the Virgin Islands, but hold that thought for a second. I need to find Gina real fast. I'll be right back to finish what we started. I promise."

I had to make up some type of excuse to get away from this man. Once I was able, the next time this fat nigga would be seeing me is when I would be hauling his fat ass off to jail. I had enough information on him that I could leave and that's exactly what I had planned to do. First I had to find Gina and tell her that I was ready to go. If she wanted to stay, then she could, but I had things that needed to be taken care of. Scoping the place out, I found her talking to some guy who she was just giggling crazy with. After Gina seen me coming her way, this bitch had the nerve to stick her nose up at me as if she didn't want to be bothered.

"Okay bitch! I'm out," I said. And that's what I did, I decided to just leave. I had done what I was supposed to do and that was to plant my seed, baby.

SHANTEL:

It had been a couple of weeks since I heard from this punk ass nigga, Hectic. He ain't made no effort to come over or even call a bitch to see if I was s breathing. I can't believe he would play his hand like this. But it was all good because he had no idea that I had seen his ass. Yeah! I had seen him and that bitch a few weeks ago at the gas station laughing it up and having a good ole time. But would things have been so funny if I had lugged out my gun and shot both of you down like the dogs they are? I didn't think so!

After a few more minutes of me talking to myself in the bedroom mirror mad as fuck, I walked to the bathroom and dropped two tablets in the searing bathwater. Before enjoying myself in the hot tub, I realized I had forgotten something in my bedroom. I rushed back to get it. I was butt naked like I loved to be in my own house. My ass swayed like a snake would do to a nice rhythmic flute melody. I was burning up inside and I needed to release this pressure between my long, lovely legs. I grabbed what I needed and before heading back to the bathroom, I also grabbed the phone.

As I stuck my well-pedicured toes into the bubbly water, Jill Scott's voice echoed throughout the house. I lay back in the Jacuzzi tub, enjoying the balmy water that covered my light brown, naked skin. I started to get into the mood and stuck my finger into my warm net. It was on fire like a California forest.

I started this small episode off with one finger and before I knew it, I was working hard with three long fingers up my juicy wet cunt. I slid one of my legs out of the water and placed it outside the Jacuzzi. I rode my hand as if I was riding the city train service. With every thrust I gave, I thought about Hectic and the way he use to pound this pussy out like a mallet to a dent. The more I thought about him the heavier my breathing started to get. The heavier I started to breath, the more I could feel myself wanting to explode all over my fingers.

Not wanting to end it like this, I grabbed the phone and dialed up Hectic's number. After getting his voice mail, I decided to leave him a little something to remember me by. I reached over and snatched up the dildo that sat on the edge of the tub and placed the rubber dick inside my deep, luscious hole. Making sure that the phone picked up the conversation my pussy was having with the rubber dick, I began to moan louder with every second that skipped by. "Oh, Hectic, this your pussy, baby. This is yours, baby. Oh, God I'm about to cum." I let out a loud scream as some of the pressure that was trapped in me like an evil spirit was released into the now warm waters.

After my heart rate went back down to its normal pace, I started to laugh, while leaving another message for this punk-ass nigga who acted like he couldn't get at me. In my sexiest voice, I said, "POP," and hung the phone up because there was nothing more to say. I was tired of this nigga.

Finally washing my ass and getting all fresh, I decided it was time to get ready for bed. I poured a small glass of red wine and read a few pages of my Ebony magazine. I could feel my eyes getting heavy like a ball and chain. Fluffing my pillows up and getting up under my favorite warm comforter, I felt under my pillow for the coldness of my pistol. And with that, I went to sleep with a smile over my face.

SUKI:

SNIIFFFF! "Damn." I savored the cocaine juices as they traveled down my throat. MMMMMMMMM! This shit was hitting like my mom's seven up Cake on Christmas. Christmas was s five months away. I look at it like this: Some loved to drink Henny. Some loved to smoke on that Kush. Some, like me and Three Six Mafia, loved to snort that white powder and everything else in between until we was on that level of no return.

I was feeling lovely and higher than a damned Catholic cathedral ceiling. This shit felt good to me because I had money to blow on this high-quality cocaine that I was sniffing off this white tramp's titties. I was now a certified nigga on getting that money and I kept that cash flowing like Derek Jeter on deck smacking homeruns for the Yankees. Wasn't no burning my money up today and coming back tomorrow with the AR15 to get your shit like I use to do when I ran with my old crew. And wasn't no more punching you in the face with the .9mm and snatching up your brand new bouncing baby boy by his shitty-ass diapers asking where the stash was at.

Now I was switching lanes in a 2010 pearl-white Land Rover LR4 HSE that I had tossed a soft 50 stacks on. I was now rocking Louie and Gucci as if I knew those pasta- eating Italians' personally. Dolce and Gabbana frames stayed wrapped around my face like Mexican tortillas stayed wrapped around beans, cheese, and beef. And I had no problem flicking off my Kush ashes on club floors while getting head from another man's bitch who couldn't keep her pretty little fingers off my zipper. I was now a luxury nigga, addicted to brown liquor, fine cocaine, and slut white bitches that took it in the ass. This was the first time in my life that I didn't care about the price of shit. Not even my own life. SNIIFFFF!

"Baby, you going to let me get some?" Damn! That's all this white bitch wanted to do. Suck my dick like a porno star, take it in every hole like a porno star, and sniff up all my damned coke like a porno star.

"Ain't you had enough yet?" I asked. The brunette white girl shifted her look towards the mountain of coke I had lying in the bed with us like an extra pillow.

She said. in a pleading voice, "But you told me if I took good care of you the whole night, then you would take good care of me the whole night, daddy."

Damn! The snowflake was right. So I decided to say, "You know what? You damned right. Now get the fuck out. We done, get your shit and bounce."

The white girl looked at me like I was crazy, then at the heap of coke and instantly tried to grab for my dick that had lost its stiff structure twenty minutes ago. I was exhausted. My dick had lost its sensitivity and shriveled up on me like a coward caught in a fucked up position. On top of that, I had to meet my nigga, Niko. Wasn't no way I was going to spend my night cooped up in the crib with this coke-sniffing, balls-licking, nut on breath guzzler. "Bitch, get out."

After sniffing a few more lines…SNIIFFFFF, I jumped my ass in the shower to get fresh from the many hours of ramming my dick in this white girl's face and partying like the world was about to end in the morning. I had dealings to take care of if I wanted to generate this money I was now in custody of. Now that I wasn't out here snatching niggas up like the Feds,

I had to find a way to recycle this money like used plastic pop bottles. I was about that money now that I finally had a lot to play with and every time a nigga saw me, I wanted a muthafucka to think I hit the lottery every week of the month. The only way I could do that was to push these packs. SNIIFFFF!

I had finally made it out to Westlake where Niko resided with some white girl that loved to strip for a small fee. I took a look in the rearview mirror to make sure that I left no evidence on the tip of my nose about this snorting habit I had picked up. After seeing that I was tight, I jumped out of the truck, feeling like a million bucks and higher than a muthafucka.

Greeting me at the door was Karen, whom I had met a few times. With her were two of her white girlfriends that also loved to strip for that same small fee at the local titty bar. As I could tell, all three girls were smoking good and drinking lovely, while watching one of the millions of reality TV shows that gleamed off the flat screen. Screaming loud as if Niko was two blocks away, Karen yelled, "Niko…your cute friend's up here waiting for you." The Heidi Klum looking, ass-white girls kept looking at me. I too stood back looking at them thinking, I could have a blast with all three of these hookers and an ounce of powder. All four of us could go hard in the paint like Dwight Howard or a young and slimmer Charles Barkley. I wanted to reach for my now semi-hard crotch. But a familiar voice that had caught my attention. Snapping out the coke spell I was under, I looked to my right and seen Niko standing in front of the basement door waving for me to come on.

Niko's basement was live and I could see why he got his chill on down here. This nigga had a black and gold bar that contained those exclusive bottles of brown and white liquor that a nigga only broke out on special occasions. He also had a sixty-five-inch plasma TV, a pool table, and some nice brown leather furniture that was soft as fresh- baked bread. Without saying one word to me, Niko walked into the laundry room and came back out with two kilos of that butter.

A brick of cocaine was going for thirty stacks and up because of the way the economy was finger fucking everyone, including the rich. Nevertheless, I was getting them at twenty-four a pop. Then, I turned around selling them for twenty eight five a brick. I refused to mess around in Cleveland because it was too damned hot to be trying to serve these dehydrated niggas. Since these cock suckers had built a Federal building downtown, the Feds was crawling around the city like cockroaches in a filthy kitchen. So I started pushing my shit to the Akron and Youngtown niggas that was trying to get paid in full.

"Grab me that fold-up table in the corner, Suki." I grabbed the table and broke that baby down like you would break down a hunting rifle. Niko then walked behind the bar and pulled out an electric knife, a digital scale, and brung it to the table to carve in the dope like a Thanksgiving turkey. I knew my train of thought was s screwed up because the thirst in my blood was kicking in full charge as I sat looking at all this dope. If I wanted to get on that, 'Get Down or Lay Down' bullshit, I could've because there wouldn't be anything Niko or those bitches upstairs could do about it to stop me from slumping all of them.

But I was trying to change my evil ways and do this the right way because I had the bread to make shit work in my favor. I was just so used to being a hustler's worse nightmare and a hard habit was just too tough to break. Feel me? SNIIFFFF!

CHAPTER 7

SNITCH:

In a Chicago hospital, I lay in the bed after my operation trying ineffectively to move. The two shots I had taken weren't as life threatening as I had first thought. However, I still suffered a broken pelvis and a broken leg in my leap to freedom from Suki's crazy-ass Nova. Waking up from the deep slumber I was under, I had felt some cold metal shit up against my sore wrist not allowing for me to move. "What the hell?" Shifting my eyes around the room to adjust to the light glaring in my face, I had to take a double take because I thought I had seen someone sitting in the corner across the room.

My eyes weren't playing tricks on me. I could see clearly that it was a police officer, sitting in a chair reading some type of magazine. "What the fuck?"

Hearing a slight mumble come from my raspy voice, the black officer reading the Sporting News on the biggest free agency in NBA history rose from his chair and left the room without saying a word to me.

A few minutes later, a white man going bald and rocking a grey goatee came through the door. He was wearing a tight, grey, three-piece suit that hugged his wiry, tall frame. "Oh, Mr. Anderson, I see that you're awake and talking. That's good. You have a lot of explaining to do. Wouldn't you say? You know, you're facing some serious charges, including first degree murder."

I had already made it clear that I wasn't going down for a murder case when I was in the back of that ambulance. "Hold the fuck up!" I protested. "I ain't killed nobody. I was brought to some shit I wasn't even trying to be a part of. Shit! You see I got two big holes in my ass along with some broken bones. I had to jump out of the car to get away from that damned lunatic. Don't' that count for something? So, you can chill on that murder shit. I ain't killed shit and you can put your last dollar on that."

I don't know what was going on in the detective's mind. But he was looking at me not saying a word. Those few seconds of silence had me panicky. The only sounds in the room at that moment were the popping of that blue gum in his mouth and this dumb- ass beeping coming from the machine that sat above me. Then this cock face reached inside of his jacket and pulled out a small notepad and began to write. He then asked me, "Well, why don't you go ahead and tell me everything that happened from start to finish? And if I get the slightest notion that you're lying to me, I mean the tiniest notion that you're lying to me, I'm going to get up and charge you with murder and I ain't playing with your black ass."

Scared to death and not faking the funk, I ended up telling the man what he wanted to hear. I told him everything from start to finish. Word to God, I told him the truth.

"So, you telling me this Dwayne Nelson out of East Cleveland, Ohio shot the old lady, drove the getaway car, and on top of that he shot you twice because you wasn't with the program?" he asked me when I had finished telling my story. I shook my head trying to reassure them that I was telling the truth and nothing but the truth. The detective gave me a quiet stare again then said, "All you niggers are the same. You know that? If you ain't snitching each other out, y'all killing each other. You muthafuckas is doing the world a big favor."

The skinny, tall, white man stood up looking at me, then turned around to leave without saying another word to me. I screamed, "You believe me don't you? Are you going to get these damned cuffs off me or what?" The detective then turned around on the back of his heels and say, "Oh, thank you for the information and you get well soon because you're black ass is still being charged with what I told him meant nothing. I couldn't believe what I had got myself caught up in. This had to be a damned nightmare that I needed to wake up from. Tears started rolling down my face as I pulled and yanked at the handcuffs holding me back from my freedom.

DAVE:

I couldn't believe what Hectic and Suki were going through. I hated to see boys that were like brothers beefing about money, honor, and power. I've known both of them since they were young and it killed me to be a witness to this sadness.

Yet, I was a hustler and what did a hustler love more than a piece of ass or a gold linked chain? He loved money and I knew for sure what me and Hectic was about to get into. And to be honest with you, I had no idea how much cash flow Suki had come across. But, I knew I had to choose sides because I had bills, luxury taxes, and a few baby mommas to look after so that they wouldn't press child support charges against a nigga. Suki not only disrespected Hectic, but he also disrespected his crew, his niggas, and his brothers of the struggle. You don't cross family out. Real always recognized real all over the world. He wasn't representing us! This nigga was representing sitting down to piss ass niggas.

Anyways, I had to call Nikki and tell her to come over because it had been almost three weeks since I had seen her. I was hoping she wasn't getting all emotional about this fat-ass nigga we was trying to put to sleep. She knew we didn't play that shit and I prayed her head was s in the game and that her intentions were still as shady as ours.

Nikki had finally arrived. It had been some time since we'd sat down and talked. Even though she was very attractive to me and thousands of other niggas who looked her way, she was like my little kid sister. Nikki still looked beautiful as when I first met her at the Greyhound bus station, crying with nowhere to lay her pretty head and nothing to put into her empty belly. Some immature punk that called himself a pimp had blackened her eye and stripped her of the little dignity she had left.

But after giving me the opportunity to speak to her and encouraging her to come with me, baby girl been good ever since. She now knew how to use men without opening her sexy long legs and she had realized that she had the gift to make men buckle at her every call. Now Nikki was pushing a 2009 BMW, had her own loft downtown, and kept money in her purse or wherever she kept her earnings.

Watching Nikki sit with her lovely legs crossed and her womanly shit together, I marveled that she had that innocent look about herself that I loved so much. I walked to the fridge and grabbed a couple cans of soda. I brought one back for her and said, "Damn! You can't get back at me? You running all over the city with this fat-ass nigga, but you ain't getting back at me? What the fuck going on?"

Nikki uncrossed her legs and put the orange soda on the table without using the coaster. She knew this bugged me. She said, "Dave, it took me longer than I thought it would take. You think I like sitting up under that nasty-ass nigga? Plus, he was too occupied about meeting some bitch named Jazz. So I had to work a bit harder and longer." I sat across from her looking to see if I could pick up on any lie that slithered from her mouth like a ravenous snake. I knew her well and it seemed that she was telling me the truth. Being in the game as long as I have, I knew that you could never trust scores of muthafuckas in this game. I hoped Nikki wouldn't ever take that part personal, but that's just the way the game went if a nigga wanted to see another day without getting his brains painted on the wall like graffiti.

Feeling a bit better about the situation at hand, I said, "So, is everything still a go?"

Nikki grabbed her soda and took a swig then said, "Yeah, everything a go, Nigga. I told you that I was the best at making these guys melt in my hands like putty."

We laughed at her statement, talked a bit longer, and then gave each other a long hug before we both left our separate ways.

I had to meet Hectic at the garage so we could strategize on getting this cheese from this fat rat and his cronies. Niggas do come back for vengeance when it comes to yanking this much paper. We wasn't trying to leave no witness to the job we was about to put down. I'll be damned if I be walking around the city having to look over my shoulder wondering if someone was trying to snuff me out because I took his shit. Everybody up in that bitch that wasn't a part of my squad was going to feel the burn.

HECTIC:

I just got off the phone with Jasmine, trying to see if she wanted to grab a bite to eat. But, she was busy and told me that she would get at me later in the night if time permitted. "Yeah, Whatever," I muttered. After talking briefly with her, I got a phone call to meet Dave at the garage because it was time to put shit in motion. Mashing the gas to catch up with him, I saw something that made me about to loose my cool.

I reached over to the passenger seat and put my hand on the .44 caliber I had hidden under today's newspaper. The white E-class 350 Benz Cool's bitch was leaning on was parked in front of some house on 102nd and St. Clair. I figured this was where she was staying. As I got closer, I seen she was chillin' with that Rasta islander I knew she was getting down with. It was all good, because I was about to scalp both of 'em right where they stood. The anger that was trapped inside of me was forcing me to grit my teeth so hard that I thought they was going to break them., I was extremely anxious to bust both these bitches up.

However, my actions were stopped in mid-deliberation.

As bad as I wanted to blow their brains out their skulls, the game god wouldn't allow for it to go down that way. Running around both of them was three, little, cute girls. They seemed to be enjoying themselves chasing colorful butterflies. There was no way that I could take shots knowing I could hit one of the small children. I wouldn't be able to live with myself if something tragic had happened to one of those girls, knowing I was the cause of it. My manhood wasn't being tested at all. It was the little morals and main beliefs I s had in this wicked body that kept me grounded. There was always tomorrow. If I didn't get my shit twisted from a nigga I did something to months ago. 'Til then, I knew where they were posted up and I would be back. Believe that shit.

Making it to the garage before Dave, I decided to take care of some business that could save us some important time. I walked over to the Caddie and popped open the trunk of the old but once-nice car and grabbed the two big black bags. Placing both of them on the floor, I then reached inside and pulled out the two chrome shotguns I had copped and began pushing the dumdums into them and bullets into the other weapons I had in the bags. I wanted to make sure that everything was on the level and the only way that I could feel comfortable was to load them myself. I didn't want to have no problems pop up when it came to snatching these dead Presidents from these niggas and when it came to snatching the faces off these studs.

I heard the side door come to life. I cocked the M-16 just in case it wasn't who I was expecting. In came Dave and his two wild ass friends talking loud about something dealing with LeBron. I was hip to these two crazed niggas he had with him. They had gone on a few licks with us before. I truly had no problem with them coming along because I knew, for a fact, that they would bust their guns. But I wished Cool were here with me to be a part of this gold mine we had stumbled across.

"That ho-ass nigga chose Miami over us and he gon' play us like that? Man, that shit ain't cool. Let me catch that nigga running around the city." Dave was mad as fuck. But, I told his ass last week that the nigga was going to leave. I knew that he was a coward and he just showed his true colors. Coward niggas always did coward shit.

"Fuck that nigga!" is what I thought, because that nigga was already paid and that's what I was trying to do. Get paid.

As I tried to speak up about hitting this lick that I was more concerned about than where the fuck LeBron was going, Dave and one of the brothers started arguing about this corny nigga. "LeBron just want some rings and he think he can't get 'em in Cleveland. How you going to get mad at that?"

Dave's face had twisted up like a head full of nappy corn rows as he said, "How I'm going to get mad? Are you fuckin' serious, dude?"

A few seconds later everyone was talking at once to the point that it sounded like niggas was about to fight. Oh, I got something for that...

POP! POP! POP...POP! POP! I had one of the M-16'd in my hand busting that bitch up in the air knowing this would get every muthafucka's attention now. With Dave's eyes big as thirty-six-inch rims, he screamed, "What the fuck is wrong with you, scaring the shit out of me like that?"

With smoke and sulfur still floating in the air, I said, "We got to get some type of understanding up in this bitch. We about to go hit this lick and y'all niggas talking about this corny ass nigga, LeBron. Fuck that nigga. Y'all got to chill with that and get focused on getting this muthafucka's money."

Dave and the two brothers started laughing at each other and knew I was right. Malik said, "Toss me something, nigga."

Fifteen minutes after everyone was on point, we all started to get dressed in the black overalls we had bought from Home Depot. Everyone had chosen the weapons they felt more comfortable with. Dave checked out the Mac .11 he had in his hands, plus the M-16 that sat next to him. Skeet was feeling the AK-47 choppa, while I had the AR-15 with the 100 round drum, plus the P-89 Ruger that I had stashed in my jacket for that extra comfort. Malik chose to take both pistol grip shotguns with him. He placed one across his back and kept one in his hands. Now that everyone was together, we sat back and fired up two blunts of some 'Silver Haze' and thought about where we wanted to be in a couple of hours.

CHAPTER 8

GINA:

I had arrived at the prison to visit Zay. I hoped Marcus and his boys hadn't said nothing to Zay about what went down at the party a couple of days ago. He would flip out on my ass if he got word I wasn't behaving myself, especially around his boys. I tried to make shit better by bringing in this weed and these few grams of coke he asked for. It wasn't like this was my first time attempting this because I had made a few moves before this. But I generally would put up a fight before giving into his spoiled ass ways. Yet, this time I chose to keep my mouth shut and give up no fight to his reasons.

As I walked into the process room, I was pleased to see it was the same officers I had dealings with before. If it would've been another officer, then the move would've been dead as Michael Jackson and his glittered glove. The dark-as-a-chocolate-bar officer looked me up and down with a smile that I was pretty sure meant he wanted to get into my panties. Flashing his sexy model smile and dimples, the eye-catching officer asked me for my purse. I was blushing so hard from his watching me that my nipples had hardened through the thin fabric of my shirt. I almost dropped my purse while handing it to him. Doing what he always did, he snatched out the package, hid it in his coat while handing the purse back to me saying, "Go on in, baby." Before entering the visiting room, I gave the officer a closer look this time and thought he was kinda cute with that uniform on. I could picture his black ass cuffing me up.

Marching into the visiting room full of convicts, snitches, cheaters, and liars, I spotted Zay in the far corner, smiling as if he hadn't seen me in years. As I got closer to him, he stood up so I could give him a warm sincere hug, letting him know that I was missing him dearly. I said, "Hey, daddy," and tried to kiss him. I was shocked when he turned away from these luscious lips. I tried to offer him. "OMG! Please don't tell me someone ran their mouth off to this damned fool," I thought.

Zay sat down and I followed him as if I was trained to do so. Before he had the chance to open his mouth, I asked him what he wanted from the vending machine. He didn't look like he was mad at me and shit. Maybe one of these rollers had him upset or something because he would tell me on the phone that the officers would fuck with some of the inmates just because they had the badge. However, he just said that he wanted a soda and that was it.

I made sure to wear something super duper tight for Zay to see this entire ass I was carrying around like Gucci luggage. This same ass that was waiting for him to get home too. Yet on my way to the vending machines, I swear I thought about turning and leaving because Zay was acting strange and I wasn't sure if he was mad at me. You supposed to always go with your first mind and I didn't. Damn!

After making it back and giving Zay the soda, I could see him shaking the plastic bottle up and just starring at me with this strange look over his mug. Finally, Zay said, "So, you out there playing me like that in front of my mans then?" He then took the cap off the soda allowing for the cold contents to splash all in my face. "Yeah, ain't this how you like it? Ain't this how you like to get down with niggas? Then you want to bust up in this bitch trying to kiss all up on me. Bitch, I ain't trying to taste no niggas babies in my mouth. Are you serious?"

Oh shit! I couldn't believe that he was playing me like this. I could see everyone in the visiting room watching us, the way Zay was clowning me. My mouth hung open like a broken zipper as he continued, "My boy told me how you was getting down at the party and how you been acting since I been gone. I should ring the alarm on your ass. But I got ninety days left in this bitch and you can keep doing you. I'm cool on yo rat ass." Then he got up and left me sitting in my chair looking real stupid and soaked thanks to a bottle of Dr. Pepper. I felt so embarrassed that I wanted to cry, but I wasn't going to do that in front of all these nosy people. They had already seen too much as it was.

Grabbing a few napkins and getting my act together, I left the visiting room with my head held high as the blue skies. However, by time I got in the parking lot, I had tears running down my face like boys and girls racing to a damned ice-cream truck. I couldn't believe I just got shitted on by this low-life ass nigga. I promised myself as I sat behind the steering wheel with two puffy, red eyes and a runny nose that I was going to fuck Jasmine up. It was her damned fault. She shouldn't have left me there.

JASMINE:

In actuality, I wanted to go out with Anthony. But, I had received a message from Petro that tonight was the night we was going to apprehend Marcus and his crew. The plan was to have two large sweeps on both sides of the city and I was to ride with the crew going to get Marcus. So, I had to get prepared to do what I did best and that was to bring animals to justice and off our streets. Putting on my game face was like putting on a fresh pair of panties when I got out the shower because these types of raids were always nerve racking to me. Reason being, you could lose your life if you wasn't careful. I always had to remember that I was dealing with dangerous criminals who wouldn't be in too much of a good mood when they seen me coming.

I got downtown and walked right into an office full of officers thirsty for some type of action tonight. Some officers lived for this type of exploit and most of the male officers fed off the adrenaline of other officers itching to have a reason to pull the trigger. I hated being around officers like that.

"I'm glad you decided to make it, Jasmine." Petro said sarcastically. He was sipping a cup of coffee and munching on a donut with red, white, and blue sprinkles all over it.

I gave him a slight smile and walked to the back of the room to finish listening to the plan the small Asian shift Captain was drawing together on the white board. With names of suspects and streets scribbled across the boards, he said, "Around three in the morning, we'll be getting into position. My resources have told me, there are three entries into the house and we'll be covering every one of them. We'll have assistance from the Cleveland police, Shaker Heights police, ATF, and FBI. So, there will be no getting away. Make sure that you're ready to react to any funny shit. These punks aren't about to just invite us in. Be careful out there. And if possible, we want all suspects in one piece. Okay?"

After hearing the plan that ended around ten-thirty, I saw that I had a few hours to relax. Warrants s had to be printed up. So, I decided to go into one of the empty offices and take me a short nap. I had a headache because now that this mission was about to be over, what was I going to do about Anthony? I really liked him and I didn't want to go back to Washington D.C. without him. Maybe it would just be easier to tell him the truth now that this was about to be over with. As a matter of fact, that's exactly what I'm going to do. I'd see him in the morning and explain.

DAVE:

We had a neighborhood fiend named Smokey who got his name from smoking everything from Newport 100's, to wet joints, then straight to that glass pipe. If the crack monster hadn't bitten him on the ass like it did an assortment of people in my neighborhood, then maybe he would've had a chance to become someone successful out the 'hood. Life, right now, was hard as a bag of jawbreakers for his ass.

Convincing Smokey to five-finger-discounts us a

conversion van for a nice piece of crack wasn't hard-hitting at all. The things a fiend would do for a flare of some bad or good dope was s unbelievable to me. But it was a sure blessing to those who was out there doing some of the wildest and weirdest shit to get a bump of that crack.

After everyone got situated inside the van and all weapons and tools that we would need for this escapade were in place, we started to make our climb up the hill towards Shake Heights to go act like damned fools.

We rode in silence as Ghost face pounded out the speakers of the old, rusted-out GMC van. Hectic sat up front with me. He had a heart like a fuckin' lion. I really wanted him to get out of this game before it got too sour for him. This way of life would eventually catch up to him or anyone else who participated for long. You was either going to get snatched up by the "One Time", or someone was going to catch you slipping and place your ass on a missing persons bulletin board. Hectic, Cool, and Suki was all good dudes. But, sometimes, life makes you do shit you really don't want to do. Didn't none of us want to grow up being homeless and living on the streets holding signs that said we would entertain for money. That was never a dream of anyone I hung out with. The pressure of having nice clothes, rides, and bitches was almost everyone's common denominator to get out there and get it the best way they knew how. And that's how niggas like me and my crew all became a product of our environment. It was a tough and rutted road. But, shit! Someone had to travel it.

After locating Marcus' house, I shut off the engine of the rusted-out GMC. In the quiet we sat in the van a few more seconds. Then Hec said, "Let's go do what we came here to do. Ain't no reason to sit around and go over no plans because the only plan is to get what we came for and lay these busters down."

The lick was supposed to go down tomorrow, but Nikki said the move was going down tonight. So we didn't want to be late for the party these niggas was putting together like Lego blocks. Inside the van you could hear the click clacking of metal as everyone made it out of the van and into the waiting arms of the crisp and brittle night breeze that shot up my pants legs. Silence was walking gracefully around this suburb like the dope fiends and wolves walked gracefully around ours. It was best to keep a watchful eye out for peeking neighbors.

Making it to the backyard without being detected by nosey neighbors who couldn't mind their business, we hid behind a few big trees that had worked out in our favor. We stood about twenty yards away from the house that looked as cozy as a sexy model in lingerie waiting for my advances.

I said, "Nikki told me the back door would be left open for us to come through. She said there would be a few security guards crawling around the house, but the main security would be on the first floor in Marcus' fat ass. So, don't get tricked into thinking everyone ain't holding some heat. We done did this shit before, so let's go take what belongs to us."

I moved first towards the back door. Hectic followed. Malik and Skeet followed in sequence. Making it to the back door with no interruption, I gave the knob a turn and watched it unlatch easily. So far Nikki was on point because the door came to life as easy as she said it would. We all slid into the darkness of the kitchen and hid behind the island that sat in the center of the colossal kitchen. We all could see that the living-room light was on. Voices bounced off the walls. People were only fifteen feet away from us.

I stuck my head around the corner of the island to look by the refrigerator. Guess what I saw? I peeped two dog bowls with food s in them. It left me to wonder where the hell the dogs were. I had an inkling that the dogs were no prized poodles and I had to whisper to everyone to be aware of them. When I finally got the nerve to look over the center island, I saw a young woman making her way into the kitchen. She was carrying an empty glass and walking towards the refrigerator. I guess she was going to get another cool refreshment. Quickly ducking my head not wanting to be spotted, I waited to see if she was going to flick on the lights. But, she didn't. At this instant, my heart began to beat fast inside my chest. I knew this was the moment to get it popping.

I rose as softly as I could and crept my way towards the opposite side of the refrigerator door. When the young, pretty girl closed the door, I immediately grabbed her by the throat smashing her lightweight ass against the wall trying to be as quiet as possible. The young girl's eyes almost popped out of her brown face. She tried to scream for help. However, the help that she was seeking wouldn't make if before this bullet exploded her pretty little head all over the kitchen walls. With a quiet pop of the .9mm with the silencer on it, I put a big hole in her head. I then slowly laid her body on the floor and waved for everyone else to step.

I peeked around the corner to try to get a glimpse of the people in the living-room. In doing so, I seen Nikki looking dead at me. I placed my index finger up to my lips, letting her know to shut the fuck up and to remain unruffled. Running my eyes across the vast living-room, I noticed some nappy-head ass nigga and another young girl playing a game on the entertainment system. Neither one of them had any idea that there would be no beating the high score tonight. Death was creeping around the corner and he wasn't taking any hostages. None whatsoever!

In crouching tiger style, me and Hectic made our way into the living-room by crawling on our hands and knees until we had made it to our destination behind the couch.

Reaching up and grabbing a handful of hair, I then put the barrel to the back of the nigga's neck and squeezed off two shots. POP! POP! Before the dark skinned girl could jump up and react to her friend's voice box shooting across the room like a shooting star, she grabbed her throat where it had been slit by Hectic. While hot liquid oozed out of the young girl's throat and down her chest, Nikki jumped up and pointed into the hallway. "There's a nigga standing in the hallway in front of the door Marcus and his friends are in." I nodded my head and told her to go wait for us in the van and have the engine on when we come running up out this bitch. Right when we were ready to make our move to silence the nigga in the hallway, everyone was frozen stuck by what waited for us at the hallway entry.

Two huge, weighty Dobermans was standing in the doorway growling low but loud enough for us to know they was about to get on some bullshit. Not giving any of us a second to think about what we were going to do, both dogs were in attack motion, running and leaping into the air like Wonder Dog. I spun around and popped one of the dogs in the head before it got the chance to get full flight. The heavy dog hit hard on the floor as it slid on the shiny wooden floors.

The second dog was in the air and on its way towards Hectic who shot the dog twice—once in its underbelly and once in the eye. This sent the dog crashing into the living-room table. This racket forced the nigga in the hallway to investigate the strange noise. We could hear his footsteps fast approaching.

Precisely when the guard stuck his head into the living-room, Malik had the shotgun on him freezing the nigga cold as an ice cube right where he stood, "Bitch ass nigga, don't say shit and get ya damned hands in the air." Skeet ran over and grabbed the .45 he had stuffed in his pants and the AK-47 he held over his head.

Malik said, "If you say anything, I promise you I'll spread your body parts all over the house like mayo on bread." Malik then turned the nigga around and forced him down the hallway. We all followed.

Malik had the guard standing in front of the door where Marcus and his friends were huddled, demanding that he open the door. "Nigga, get this door open or I'll blow your spine through your mouth. Now try me." The young guard was so scared that he couldn't stop shaking. He had farted about three times that I could count alone. I knew he was scared and probably thought if he did what we asked he would get a chance to leave here in one piece. Maybe he was right and then maybe he was wrong.

Malik had the shotgun jammed in the back of the petrified guard. Me and Skeet stood to one side of the door and Hectic stood on the other side. We could hear the laughing and giggling behind the door. We all knew this was now or never because wasn't no coming back after this.
Malik nudged the kid in the back and told him to open the

door. Once the door had finally opened, all eyes were now on us and our disastrous wretched ways.

Without second guessing himself, Malik put a big hole in the young kid's back. BOOM! The explosion pushed all the young kid's guts and horrible insides on the face of the two Detroit boys. This alone had one of Marcus' boys jump fly and play hero. Malik right now was in that kill zone and spun around and hit the hero-ass nigga twice. He shot off one of his arms and parted his broad chest open like the Red Sea. Everyone else in the small room froze up like fruit popsicles and got a real understanding about what the fuck was taking place.

"Who the fuck is y'all and what the fuck y'all want?" Hectic leaped over the dead body of the young kid and smacked Marcus up side his head with the P-89. WHACK!

"Shut the fuck up, nigga. You know what time it is? As a matter of fact, get your fat ass up." While Skeet and I tied up everyone with grey duct tape, Hectic tied Marcus, whipping his ass at the same time.

On the floor lay three big duffle bags and on the table sat two silver suitcases that I was sure held money. Hectic and Skeet opened up the three bags. Two of them contained ten bricks each. The other bag contained forty pounds of Kush bud. After seeing what we had, Hectic rushed to zip the bags back up and told Malik to rush one of the bags to the van and that we would be right behind him. Malik did what he was told.

I snatched up the two silver suitcases and Hec snatched the other two bags up.

In all, there was four niggas laid out on the floor wondering what the hell was going to happen to them next because we said nothing else to them as we jetted out the room.

However, there was nothing to talk about because we did this move with no ski masks on. So they had to have an idea about how this story was going to end.

After we ran from the room, Skeet rose off the wall with the AK-47 choppa in hand and gave everyone a devilish grin before he riddled the small office with empty shells, pieces of body parts, and puddles of young black men's blood. What was already understood didn't need to be explained.

As me and Hectic strolled outside into the brisk cold air trying to make it to the van, we both saw a strange figure lying in the grass not moving. Without hesitation, Hectic put down the two bags, pulled out his handgun, and walked up to the strange figure not moving in the grass. Hectic was confused. I ran up to see what had him fixed on this silhouette and couldn't believe what the hell I was looking at. It was Malik's lifeless body lying in the grass with a knife stuck deep inside of his cranium. And to top that off, the bag he had with him was nowhere in sight. What the fuck?

"What y'all looking at?" Skeet said running up behind us. When he seen his brother laying on the ground with a big ass hunting knife sticking out his head, he said nothing. I mean absolutely nothing. He dropped the -hot choppa to the cold ground and picked up his brother and carried him to the van. Me and Hectic was at a loss for words. We both looked towards the van, grabbed the bags, and ran for it.

When we finally made it to the van, it was empty. Nikki was nowhere in sight. Hectic dropped both bags and threw his hands in the air and said, "I told you not to trust that bitch, Dave. This bitch just crossed us out. That could've been you or me lying in that damned backyard."

He was right. I couldn't believe that this bitch had just crossed me out like this. All I had done for her and this was the thanks I got? I looked around and seen a few lights starting to come on in the giant houses we were surrounded by. I said, "We'll find out who that bitch crossed us out with, but right now we got to get the fuck out of here."

We drove in silence once again. Skeet sat in the back far corner holding his big brother, saying nothing 'til we was back in the city. "Someone going to pay for this and I promise that. Once y'all find out who did this, make sure y'all come tell me. I'll take care of the rest," he finally told us.

CHAPTER 9

JASMINE:

I was riding in the car with three other officers when I started to get butterflies in my stomach. I s got nervous about going on raids like these types because I was never sure if I would be coming out alive and that scared the shit out of me every trip. Checking my equipment again for the thirtieth time to make sure that I had everything that I needed, I quickly closed my eyes and put my small prayer in to the Man Upstairs. "Please God," I prayed, "let me make it out alive. Please protect me from the evil that lurks inside this house. Amen."

When I lifted my head up, I could see that we we're very close to the location we were supposed to be at. My position was with the Cleveland police and I had to lead them through the back door. Other officers had the side door surrounded as well as the front. My radio sprang to life. The Asian Captain was on the other end saying, "All units in position?" I looked behind me and noticed my team of white officers, guns already drawn, ready to put some slugs into any young black male that hesitated to not listen to one command being spit out their mouths.

Finally the call came for us to move in. I told the others to lay low and to be quiet as we headed towards the back door. Opening the back door, we entered the kitchen with no struggles. However, we were all greeted by a young girl who lay motionless on the kitchen floor, part of her mouth missing.

I rushed my team into the living-room. We were all stopped once again by the lifeless bodies of one black male and female, plus a couple of dogs that got shown no mercy in the small bloodbath. A skinny white officer from the Shaker Heights Police Department said, "What the fuck happened in here?"

Before I could give him an answer to the question I had no answer for, another voice from in the hallway came screaming, "In here." I ran towards the hallway where the officer was standing. I almost threw up from what I saw.

This room was riddled with bullet holes and torn-apart bodies. I looked over the room and tried to recognize some of the bodies. There were a few I knew. I had seen the two Detroit boys. I also discovered Marcus leaning against the wall with half his face gone and his intestines hanging out of his enormous belly. He had over ten bullet holes in his body. They looked like swollen up mosquito bites. Not a pretty sight!

Petro came in with a handkerchief covering his big nose and mumbled, "Jasmine, what the hell happened here? This was supposed to be a drug bust not a damned massacre." He looked around one more time and gagged at the sight of the twisted-up, blooded bodies. "Do you have any idea who could've done this?

And if not, then I want you on top of this starting right now." I looked over the room. I had no idea who could've done this. But, I knew their reasons because there was no money or drugs in sight. How in the hell was I going to solve this? I figured after all the investigations were processed and done, I'd then take a look at the reports and go from there. All of a sudden, I had another bad headache.

SUKI:

I was sitting at a table in a club called the "Gotcha". It harbored nothing but the meanest thugs looking for any type of weakness in a nigga so they could pounce on his ass and take his belongings. But a nigga like me wasn't worried about that riff raff because they knew who to try and who not to try. And they knew that I was one of the ones to avoid because someone was going to be bleeding from a multitude of bullet holes if they messed with me.

I sat waiting for this bitch to hurry on and pick up what I owed her ass. I was in a position in my life right now that I didn't need to hit no licks. But, anything to get at Hectic and Dave was a straight up plus for me. I knew this bitch wasn't going to say shit for the simple reasons being her ass would be found in Lake Erie floating around like a dead Bluegill.

After I ordered another drink, in comes who I been waiting all night for. I raised my drink in the air, and this sexy female walked with heavy velocity towards me. She sat straight across from me and began speaking nervously, "Suki, give me my cut so I can get the fuck out of town. I want to leave town tonight."

I took a sip of the brown liquor smoothly as I gazed at this scanless bitch. I didn't really trust her because if she would cross out her homies then…But, at the same time, for the past year, I was tapping that ass and sticking my dick all in her mouth behind everyone's back. So maybe I would be the lucky one she wouldn't try to cross.

"Baby, hold ya horses. You fucking with a muthafucka. Don't bitch! Ain't nobody going to lay one hand on you. Matter of fact, take this drink and chill for a minute. You getting me all nervous and shit. You coming up in here fucking up the vibe I had going on. Damn! We'll take care of that business soon as you're done with that drink," I reassured her.

We ended up being there for only a few seconds more because Nikki took the drink and downed it right on the spot as if she ain't had a drink in years. Checking out her actions, I could tell that she was really shaken by tonight's event.

We made it out to my truck and to be honest, I too was looking around to see if anyone was lurking in the dark across of the parking lot. I wasn't concerned about these cats standing around. I was concerned about Nikki setting my ass up just like she did Hectic and Dave. This bitch just showed me that she couldn't be trusted at all. Anyhow, once we got into the truck, I took off towards Superior not really knowing where I was going. "Suki, where in the hell you taking me too? I just want my money, nigga. I don't want to lounge up, watch no movies, eat, or none of that shit. I just want my ends."

I didn't say one word to Nikki because my whole intention was to just blast this bitch right in her head. But I couldn't do it in my truck. Fuck! I had to change my plans so I said, "The money at my crib. I'm about to take you there." She knew I was staying out in Euclid, so I had to take that route so she wouldn't get suspicious of my behavior.

Me and Nikki had been cool for a long time. We had started fucking each other about a year ago. Damn! Her body was banging like the Crips and Bloods back in the late 80's. I mean, she had all the potentials a nigga would be looking for in a stunning woman. Pussy was good. Head was the bomb. She was a beautiful muthafucka, but her loyalty was always in question. Plus, she wasn't my type because she wasn't going anywhere anyways. It was really over with before it even got started. However, she didn't know that.

No one in or outside the crew had any idea about me and Nikki's late night escapades, and we weren't trying to enlighten no one either. A few weeks ago, while she was lying up in my bed after I tore that ass up, she had mentioned to me that she wanted to break away from the crew because she wanted to venture off to New York City. Why she wanted to go there, I really had no idea. But, she told me that she was tired of being in Cleveland, sort of like the same shit that other broad named LeBron told America on national television. So, she told me about this lick with Dave and Hectic. All I had to do was give her nice cut of the loot if everything had gone the way we had expected. Except there was one thing wrong with this equation: I wasn't about to giver her shit.

At last we got to my crib. After legging her in, I asked her if she wanted a cold drink or something. She shot back at me in anger, "Suki, I just want my money and stop playing games with me."

Shit! I tried to buy some time to think about how I was going to scam her. But, she was trying her hardest to fuck up my concentration. So, I sat down on the couch and did what I did best when I needed to get my thoughts in place. I pulled out a quarter ounce of coke and poured the contents on the table. I really needed a blast. Then, maybe, I could make up my damned mind about how I was going to trick this bitch into letting me ghost her ass. Not pushing a thin line together, I just stuck my whole nose in the pile of powder and. SNIIFFFF!

Wiping my nose clear of the white residue, I looked up to give Nikki a grin. To my amusement, she had a look on her face that I wasn't feeling too comfortable with. When I went to stand up, Nikki pulled out a pretty .357 on my ass. "Nigga, I told you to stop laying all these games with me. I crossed out some guys I shouldn't have and now I'm trying to get the fuck out of town before they find me. I don't have the time and patience to be playing with you, boy."

I had my hands up in the air in a joking manner and said, "Okay, baby. Let me go get your shit before you go postal up in this bitch." As I turned around to head towards my bedroom, I could feel her and that meaty .357 following right behind me. Neither, Nikki nor that gun was going to prevent me from trying her muthafuckin' ass s. I wasn't going to make this easy for her. Before entering my bedroom, I tried my luck and pulled out a chrome .45 as I spun around on her ass. POW! Damn! Nikki was faster than me. I saw the big flash coming towards me.

The hot slug hit me in the shoulder faltering my ass towards the hallway wall dropping me to the floor. The pain was stinging like a thousand hornets. I said, "Oh shit! Bitch, you shot me."

Nikki s had the smoking gun pointed towards me. She

said, "Nigga, you got me fucked up. Now if you don't get my shit, I swear I'll kill your sorry ass and get it myself."

I looked up at Nikki and knew she was serious this time. "Okay, I got you, baby," I assured her. "Damn!" I swore, as I inspected my bleeding shoulder. She walked over and picked up my gun. Now she had had both pistols pointed at my high ass.

I had got up off the hallway floor and wavered into my bedroom where I had a hidden safe in my closet. I looked back at Nikki and seen she was sweating and not looking too attractive at this point. I turned back around and started opening the safe for this scanless bitch. 24 right, 39 left, 9 right. When I opened the safe up, I snatched out fifty thousand and threw it on the bed. "Here you go." Nikki walked over to the bed and looked at the money and said, "Nigga, this ain't no hundred thousand and I'm not leaving without my money."

Ewww, this bitch was really working my damned nerves. I told her, "This all I got right now. We just hit the fuckin' lick a few hours ago. You know we didn't get the money like we had planned. I gotta sell some of this shit first, girl."

Nikki stared at me as if studying me for a lie. After a few seconds, she seemed to relax a bit because she knew I was right. "You ain't shit, nigga," she said. That part I had to agree with her. She bent over to pick up the money and toss it into her purse, taking her pretty brown eyes off me. Big mistake, bitch!

I grabbed the Calico that sat by the gold Rolex and the hundred thousand I had, and popped Nikki's ass in the middle of her back as she tried to walk out of the bedroom with my fifty thousand. POW! The fat slug tore a hole in her back. I watched blood spill out of it like a ripe, squeezed tomato. Both pistols flew from her small hands. I jumped over the bed, charging her injured ass. "Yeah, what the fuck you thought?" I looked down at Nikki as she stared at me. Blood and spit mixed together in the corner of her pretty mouth. "Did you really think I was going to allow you to leave with my money?"

I could see the pain in her face. She decided to leave me a little something in her response. She dug down deep inside her dying body and spit right in my face. The blood and spit splashed hard on the tip of my nose and lips. I didn't flinch one bit at the nasty shit. Instead, I took the tip of my tongue and licked the blood and spit off my lips as if it was barbeque sauce. Nikki wanted to say something to me. However, the pain she was feeling in her back from the burnt hole I left in her ass wouldn't allow her to get one syllable out.

I was tired of wasting my time and patience with this silly-ass bitch. I had things to do and people to meet. So, I pointed the Calico at Nikki's attractive face and pulled the trigger twice. POP! POP! I shot her in the forehead twice and watched all the beauty in her body escape like the great Houdini escaping from a bundle of chains. Grabbing the Fendi purse that lay next to her lifeless body, I snatched up the fifty stacks and wrapped Nikki and our past up in some sheets from the hallway closet. Once again, I had prevailed. It seemed nothing or no one was going to stop me. Now all I had to do was get this bullet out of my ass. But, first I needed a snort.

GINA:

I felt something fleshy slapping me in the face. When I finally opened my eyes, it was this nigga slapping me with his dick. "Yeah, go ahead and suck me off before I go to work, Ma," he said.

I whispered with sleep still in my eyes, "You won't let a bitch get up and brush her teeth or nothing, huh?"

This thirsty-ass nigga said, "I got your fluoride and toothbrush right here all in one."

I laughed and took him in my mouth. I couldn't lie. He tasted just as good in the morning as he did at night.

After I delighted him with my lips and tongue, he started to put on his work uniform. Yeah, I ended up staying the night with the officer from the prison where Zay punk-ass was at. After I left the visiting room feeling and looking a straight mess, the sexy officer who always gave me the googly eyes took a strong concern for me and my well-being. I guess he thought he was running some type of game on me. But I was really the one running the game.

My whole strategy was to get Zay back and I was willing to do that at any cost. I refuse to let this nigga come out here and take care of some other bitch while I sat back and watched. Therefore, I was going to fix his little red wagon.

I lay in the king-sized bed watching this cornball get dressed, laughing inside the whole time. It was hilarious how tender dick some of these hardcore ass niggas really was! To be honest, those were the type of men I loved to get over on. This nigga didn't have no money to satisfy my shopping habits. He didn't have a nice spot to live in, and there was no future for us at all. But this police-ass nigga did have a role to play for me and I was going to let him play it.

"Okay, baby. I'll call you when I get off work and I'll make sure that I take care of that for you. Make sure that you lock up before you leave." He blew me a kiss and I pretended to grab hold of it, 'til he closed the door behind him. I slammed his kiss to the floor like a bowl of cold oatmeal and got out of bed to shower before leaving.

While drying my hair, I turned on the TV to catch the news. To my surprise, I seen Marcus' house. I grabbed the remote to turn up the volume. The news reporter said something about Marcus and some type of massacre. Police said they had no suspects at this moment, but it was rumored that Marcus was dead. I couldn't believe that he was dead! I had just seen his fat ass a few days ago. It just goes to show you that you don't know when your last days will be on this earth and that's why you had to live for the moment and not tomorrow. Well, that was my theory on life. I can't speak for everyone else.

After getting dressed, I tried to call Jasmine but the bitch voicemail came to life leaving me wanting to beat her ass even more. As an alternative, I decided to call my crazy two friends that I really needed to converse with. They were going to love me for the small treat I had in store for them.

CHAPTER *10*

HECTIC:

Several days had gone by as I hung out cooped up in my apartment like a bird cooped up in its grubby cage. For the duration of that time, I stayed super glued to each news channel the city had to offer to see what evidence these cops had come across and what they claimed to have confirmed to the public. I knew, for a fact, that not one shred of evidence was left from our sinful raid—unless you wanted to reckon the gruesome chaos we left behind. Other than that, I knew we were clean as a whistle.

On the contrary to all this bullshit, I was s enraged at the move Nikki had put down on us and the way that Malik's life was taken like a thief in the middle of the night. The whole move wasn't supposed to have gone down like that. This move was supposed to have been as smooth and swift as a razorblade. However, we got ganked when we was the ones supposed to be doing the ganking. This shit wasn't sitting easy with the kid. Just do the math.

Right now, we were presumed to be sitting on twenty of those things, four hundred thousand, and about forty pounds of that Kush. But we had come up shorter than a midget trying to touch the floor from a highchair. We had to make right by what we did snatch up. Nigga's mugs hung low like neighborhood kid's clothes who wore their pants hanging off their asses. What could we do about it except find out who Nikki was tied into and handle that business.

Dave had come over earlier with Smokey to test out the quality of the coke. We had and a smoker sat explaining to me that he had smoked dope from Maine to Spain. This fiend-ass nigga was now geared up to try out the merchandise. I rocked up an eight ball and watched as Smokey went to work doing what he did best. He reached inside the pockets of his dirty jeans and pulled out a soiled handkerchief, which concealed his prized smoker's pipe. After unwrapping it carefully, he then broke off a piece of the crack and placed a finicky-sized stone in the pipe. Looking around at us and licking his now soggy lips, he then grabbed his Bic lighter and gave the rock some life. One puff, two. Two puffs, three. Three puffs and Smokey was stuck in place leaning his head back. Out of nowhere, he just dropped his award-winning pipe. I wanted to laugh at this jokester. But, at the same time, I didn't know what the fuck was going on with him 'til Smokey said, "Young blood, I can't feel my whole body. What the fuck ya'll give me?"

Me and Dave laughed out loud now that we knew Smokey was okay and that we had us some good coke. Now all we had to do was put this to the streets and let the streets do what it did. Sell itself.

I made a few phone calls. One was to Jasmine. But, she said that she had to go out of town again and that she would call me later on. That was cool with me because I had things to take care of too and her not being around to sidetrack me was dandy. I called Janaia and told her to meet me at the garage where me, and Dave would be in about an hour. First, I needed to run over to Skeet's house to take him and Malik their cut from that lick that was way off the mark we had set. I knew Malik wasn't here with us no more. But he was family and we didn't cross family. We just didn't get down like that. His brother was still here and that's where his cut would go.

Skeet resided on the Westside of the city on Denison over top of a corner store that stayed laced up with some Puerto Rican cats. They had the notion that Daddy Yankee could put some hip into their hop. I grabbed the .45 and placed it inside my jeans and walked my way towards the store with my leather bag over my shoulder ready to put one in a Rican's hip if he was in fact ready to hop. I didn't trust any muthafucka I couldn't understand.

Feeling no intimidation from the outlandish faces and strange language barrier, I continued my stroll up to Skeet's front door. I heard Bob Marley banging heavy on the other side of the flap. So, I knocked extra hard for Skeet to hear me. Cracking the door up with no hesitation or care about who it may have been, Skeet stood there looking at me. He was wearing some Army fatigues.

I walked into the small apartment that had its own strange warmth. The place could've taken a nice little spring cleaning from what I could smell. However, the stench wasn't what caught me off guard. It was the AK-47 that was used in a helluva slaughter a few days ago. I knew from looking at that scene that I couldn't be chillin' over here too long because the nigga was trying to go to jail for a long damned time.

"I brought you Malik's cut." I had four bricks, two hundred thousand, and ten pounds of Kush in the leather bag. Money and all that material shit was cool, but friendship is forever and I was taught that a long time ago, growing up in the streets. Spinning around checking that Skeet wasn't paying me any attention, I noticed this nigga was too focused on firing up what looked like a dipped cigarette with that damned embalming fluid dripping from it. Oh shit!

"I don't need all that shit, Hec." He stopped talking to take a deep hit of that devil's water. He blew the thick grey smoke out of his weary lungs and continued, "Give me my cut and you keep the rest. 'Cause where I'm about to go, huh, nigga can't use that shit, baby." Skeet was a hundred percent right about that speech there. Where he was about to go, he sure in the hell didn't need this or nothing else, as a matter of fact. I knew plenty of guys that smoked on that shit two years ago and s ain't come back from that wild high yet. So, I wasn't about to try to convince this crazy nigga to take this money and shit. I just wanted to bounce before he started tripping and doing some not cool shit.

I zipped up the bag and turned around to march out the front door as quickly as I could. Skeet yelled, "Hold up. I want you to check something out." Damn! So close! I almost made it out the crib before this nigga started acting all goofy and shit. I know this nigga about to be on some bullshit, I know it.

I eyed him suspiciously, hoping he wasn't about to try

to play with that rifle, I continued to watch him as he walked towards the closet to retrieve something. After a few seconds of moving things around, Skeet finally reappeared with something. My eyes had to be playing a cruel joke on me. This crazy ass nigga was carrying something out the closet that looked similar to a body wrapped up in some clear plastic wrapping like a damned hoagie sandwich. Getting a better look at what he had in his hands, it was now clear to my recognition that my eyes wasn't playing tricks on me. This nigga had Malik wrapped up like a Xmas gift. This was my cue to bounce. Peace.

JAILHOUSE ROCK:

Zay was in the backroom playing poker with six other convicts trying to pass the time and get paid all in one. "Nigga, I fold," said one of the cats sitting in the small cigarette smelled room trying to come up.

Zay took a peek at his cards and gave them another overlook to make sure his choice was the right one, and then said, "I raise fifty more dollars." This caused another to fold. He knew he didn't have fifty dollars to be tossing away. The next player in line called the fifty and raised it with another fifty. Zay looked at the half-breed looking-ass nigga, then back at his hand and said to himself, he got to have the wheel to beat my hand. Fuck it! "I call nigga." The pot was well over four hundred dollars cash and Zay felt this half-breed nigga was trying to buy the pot or trying to scare him away from that pot of gold. No matter what, Zay wasn't about to back down. Zay stood up with a Black & Mild stuck between his lips like a stick in mud and said, "Turn out, cuz."

The nigga who they called Green Eyes turned out a 3,4,5,6 and that right there wasn't going to make him a winner because Zay had a 2,3,4,5. A Kool-Aid smile came across Zay's face as he realized he was the one with the winning hand. It required him to rack up all the money and stick the crumbled bills into a Newport carton box.

Just before the next hand was about to be dealt, this little old white female officer who loved for black inmates to pull out their cocks and masturbate on her, came into the room asking for Zay.

"You need to come up to the desk. Some yard dogs are out here for you. I have no idea what they want, suga, but you need to get to the desk." She then turned around and walked out the room. As she left, she smiled at one of the intimates whose cock she done seen dozens of times.

Zay stood up and pulled out a half-ounce of crack and a quarter sack of weed and passed it off to his boy who also held an ice pick up his sleeve just in case they didn't know how to act when losing.

Approaching the desk and the three officers that was waiting for him with mad attitude, Zay said, "What the fuck is the problem and what the fuck ya'll want with me at the desk?" A tall white officer said, "We need to shake down your bed area. We don't want to hear your lip because it came from the Captain's office." Zay looked the wannabe top cops up and downs, and then says, "Let's roll." He knew he had nothing to hide from the others. He also knew that he was sparkling clean. Yet, he wondered who the hell was telling on him. Every time he got something into the prison walls, he made sure to show love to everyone just so no one would tell on him. But it never mattered how much you looked out for homies, someone still was going to tell because it was in their snitching blood. Rat bastard!

The black officer that he did his business with in the visiting room said, "Open up your box, and then step away." Zay couldn't believe this nigga was with these top cops. But, at the same time, he knew the nigga had to do his job. Doing what the officer asked Zay glanced over towards his bed noticing the other two officers tearing up his bed by pulling his sheets off the hard plastic mat and snatching his velour to the floor. They didn't find anything in particular. Zay then said, "Now can y'all leave me the fuck alone?" The three officers glared at him before turning around and walking back towards the desk. Just before Zay was ready to relax, he heard something that forced his heart to beat a little faster than normal. "Wait," screamed out the black officer as he turned around to walk back towards the bed.

Staring at the black officer wondering what the fuck he had forgotten, Zay watched as the black officer grabbed his pillow and started tearing it apart. When the officer found what he was looking for, he then turned around and smiled at Zay with a puzzling grin. That grin told Zay that someone had just set him up.

When the tall white officer told him to turn around to be cuffed up, Zay threw a punch to the thin lips of the officer and ran out the door as if he had many of options for getting away.

The officers surrounded Zay outside as he threw blows at the air hoping to hit any officer who stepped in range. "I was set up. You bitches set me up. That shit ain't mine! Fuck y'all." When Zay had tired himself out from the empty blows and empty threats, he dished out to any officer who ran up on him, the officers rushed him quickly. Zay's retreat spoke volumes as the officers beat his ass down.

Zay discovered that someone had planted an ounce of crack in his pillow. He was going to be charged with possession. That, alone, was going to add a few more years to the ninety days he had left. This fucked with him emotionally, but also psychically as he felt the broke ribs in his thin body.

The black officer that was getting two hundred in his pocket for every ounce he brought into the prison was now dragging Zay to the hole with more force than what was really needed. Subsequent to tossing Zay on the floor like a sack of rotten potatoes, the black officer whispered to him, "Gina got some good pussy and she sends her love, nigga." He slammed the door hard and walked away. Everyone in the hole could hear Zay screaming obscenities to any person who would care to pay attention to his cries.

DAVE:

An open brick of coke was spread across the wooden table like a naked chick prepared and eager to give up her secret spots without a single struggle. I had a blue bandana wrapped around my nose and mouth like a Compton gang banger so I wouldn't be inhaling the coke particles that floated around the garage as I chopped into it. Even though I was out in the streets buck wilding and acting all crazy and shit, I still had nine months of probation left and I wasn't trying to catch no cocaine dirty. My probation officer, Ms. Dunken, didn't care too much about me pissing dirty on some weed. It was the other shit like coke, PCP, and heroin that would get a brother in a muggy situation.

Anyways, earlier today, I had taken two of the bricks over to our block in East Cleveland so my homies over there could get some of this money too. We never forgot where we came from, even though we wasn't holding up those corners and running through the cuts to get away from the police anymore. But Page was home and a nigga could never forget about home even if it brought back some sad memories.

I stood for a minute watching the young cats shooting dice and run up on cars and fiends whose palms was filled with cash willing to purchase illegal items from them. It had been several months since I been down here, but as I could tell, everything was still the same around this way. People was still sitting on the front stoops of the fatigues buildings drinking and smoking, while keeping a good eye out on their stash, junkies, and the police who sometimes tried to storm the block like grey, rain clouds.

I always showed my respect to the young cronies whose older brothers I ran either the streets with or their older sisters whom I was once pounding out. After screaming out my shout outs, I found myself running up the pissy-smelling hallway stairs two at a time ignoring the crack smoke that was floating in the air. Arriving at the door I was in search of, I gave it a hard knock. BOOM BOOM! I heard the chains unlatch from behind the heavy doors. I was now face-to-face with Tameka. She looked me up and down, a glass of green Kool-Aid in her hand. She screamed with a high-pitch, "Tank, Dave out here waiting on your ass."

I walked inside the homey apartment I could smell the fried chicken, weed, and incense entwined in the air. I watched Tameka sit back on her fat ass to finish watching some rap video. I wanted to say something to her. But, I changed my mind as Tank came out of the back room. "What up Dave?" he called. "How you doing, nigga? I hope everything okay." I met him halfway and we gave each other a brotherly hug and grip before conversing.

Before getting into the state of our business, Tank says, "What's up with Suki? Why he acting all secretive and shit? I mean he was fucking with Dirty late last night and didn't say shit to me when I pulled up."

My antennas instantly went up. I said, "What you mean fucking with Dirty?"

Tank walked over to the coffee table and grabbed a cigarette. "Suki rode down in that fresh Range and pulled Dirty to the side handing that nigga a bag of something. Then later on that night, Dirty came out on the block serving us whatever we wanted," he said. "That nigga had weight for the weight boys and dubs for the dub boys and the fiends going crazy over it like if that shit some of that 80's coke. You know what I'm saying? Like some of that Miami vice Crocket and Tubbs coke. Come on, me and you both know that nigga lost his connect and style years ago. That nigga played out like MC Hammer."

I couldn't believe what I was hearing and I was stuck in my own stands trying to think and replay what Tank had just told me. Tossing the brown bag that I had in my hands onto the couch with Tameka, I then said, "Where that nigga Dirty at?"

Tank lit up the square and said, "I ain't seen that nigga since last night, Dave." I was now in a rush and had an urgency to make it to the garage to tell Hectic what the fuck I was just clued-up on. Suki was the traitor who had crossed us out with Nikki. I knew in my heart that it was that grimy ass nigga. I just didn't want to let Hectic know how I was feeling already knowing the bad blood between them. But I believe he already had the same assumption as I did. "Check this out. Its two bricks in there for you. When you done give me a ring. 'Til then, don't say shit to Dirty about you telling me about him and Suki, okay?" I said, hurriedly departing.

I don't know what was taking Hectic so long to get here, but I was almost done cutting and bagging all this shit up, plus I couldn't wait to see his face when I told him about Suki. I still couldn't put my finger on it why Suki had it in for Hectic. I mean we all been best friends for years and for this nigga to turn Bishop on us was straight up crazy to me and I couldn't figure the shit out.

Hearing the door open and close, I thought it was Hectic, but instead, it was Janaia. She was totally different from Nikki's dumb ass. The dim-witted bitch just showed all of us her true colors by the move she put down the other night. On the other hand, Janaia had her shit together. She was polished up like a brand new brass headboard. She didn't fuck with no one and she didn't play no games when it came time to do what she did best. I never saw her in action, but I heard plenty of stories about her and the way that she handled herself. I had sworn to myself a long time ago to always watch her ass and to never take my eyes off her. Right when I was about to ask her if she had talked to Hectic, he comes walking through the door.

He walked up to Janaia and gave her a kiss on her cheek then tossed his leather bag on the couch saying, "Yo! Ya boy ill. Ya boy need some help because he had Malik up in the crib wrapped up in sandwich wrap. Straight talk, Dave. I went over there and tried to give him his cut and that nigga was on some other shit. I caught ya boy smoking that gorilla piss and on top of that, he living with a damned corpse. You got some strange ass friends."

I walked over grabbing the leather bag that I seen s had two birds in it and placed them on the table with the rest of the coke. Then I said, "Suki the one who fucked us over with Nikki."

Hectic stood frozen in his tracks for a second because I guess he thought I said something else or hoped I said something else. Looking at me crazy, then he said, "What you just say? I know you ain't talking about what I hope you ain't talking about."

I grabbed my blue bandana and electric cutter and said, "Yeah, that nigga went down on the block and dropped some of that shit down on Dirty. Tank said the fiends was going wild over the shit."

Hectic rubbed his eyes, and then scratched his head and said, "What! I can't believe this dumb ass nigga would go this far to jack us. Did this nigga forget that we burn them on the regular? Did he actually forget how we got down? He got to go, Dave. He gotta go."

I could tell Hectic was mad as hell because he didn't stay long at all. He didn't inquire one thing about the dope. His channel of communications was short and directly to the point.

He said something to Janaia while giving her some money, and then he bounced. However, he was right. We had to take care of Suki and we both knew that. This nigga honestly believed that his ass is untouchable and we got to be the ones to show him that a nigga could lay hands on him.

CHAPTER *11*

JASMINE:

I was lounging in my apartment trying to figure out what the hell had gone down at Marcus' spot and who could've done this devilish crime. Well, of course anyone could've done this, but who would've had the balls to run up in there like that? I was sure it was someone who had done this plenty of times because these insane hoodlums showed that their hearts was cold as ice by the way they left the place looking.

This damned case was driving me crazy and right now I just wanted to be in Anthony's arms. I knew deep down inside that I shouldn't have these types of feelings for him. It wasn't like I was going to be able to stay here and carry on a relationship with him. I lived in Washington DC and that's where I called my home. Yet, I also knew that you couldn't help who you fell for either, and I was fallen hard for this man. Maybe I should latch another lie onto the other ten that I had told him just to leave him alone, then hurry and try to finish this job so I could just leave with no sad songs to be played. What was I going to do?

I stared at the unpleasant pictures of these bodies twisted up like knots in yarn for another fifteen minutes. Then, I decided to get up and get my ass in the shower before I jumped in my soft bed. I was really tired and my head was killing me from all the thoughts I had running around it. While taking off my blouse, I heard my cell phone ringing in the distance. In no rush to answer it, I finally grabbed the undersized mechanism. "Hello."

At first I didn't know who it was 'til I heard, "Oh! Now you can speak to a bitch. I've been trying to get in touch with you for the past three days to ask your ass a question. Why the fuck you leave me at Marcus' party like that?"

I ain't gonna lie. I was stuck for a minute because this hoodrat of a girl had the nerve to try to check me. She strictly had another thing coming. "Let me tell you something young lady, I'm not your babysitter or your mother and I did try to get you. You're the one that was acting all high society and snobby, so I left. And the reason why I ain't been answering my phone is because I have a J.O.B. Now, is that cool with you?"

Gina sat on the other end of the phone with her a long face. She knew I was right. "Pick your face up, bitch," is what I was thinking as I listened to the silence on the other end of the phone. Gina knew she was barking up the wrong damned tree and got smacked right in her face for trying to run that dumb ass shit on me.

Finally, Gina said, "Yeah, you're right and so what. But let me tell you this: Don't let me catch your bright high yellow ass out in these streets because if I do, it's going to be me and you doing the damned thang. Trust me when I tell you that. You're the reason me and Zay ain't together right now."

I wanted to bust out in laughter because I knew I could kick this bitch ass. But I wasn't a child and I had no time for her childish games, so I said, "How in the world am I the reason that you're not with your man? You're the one running the streets doing what you do. Don't put your mishaps on me because you can't keep your legs closed. As a matter of fact," I said nothing else to her stubborn ass and just hung the phone up. I had a job to do and that's what I was going to do. Fuck that duty ass bitch.

After hanging up, I rushed to the shower as if this would be my last one this year. I left a trail of clothes from my bedroom through the hallway, and all the way to the bathroom. Turning on the hot water, I automatically closed my eyes and allowed the water to run over my exposed body like a thousand hungry fingers touching my naked skin. Grabbing the soap with an exhausted hand, I began to lather myself. The lathered soap felt good on my bare skin. Ewww! I was getting in the mood to massage myself in places that were wrong. I mean a place that a Nun would disagree with me and my sinful ways a hundred percent, a place that I imagined Anthony putting his face at every night before I fell asleep, and a place that I now had the showerhead running up against.

Pressing the heaviness of the water on my clit, I began to go wild. I started gyrating my hips with a nice melody and rubbing my nipples with my free hand. In a matter of seconds, I came so hard that I almost fell against the glass shower door. I was on fire and this pussycat needed to be tamed. I knew what strong black man could tame this baby.

CAUGHT SLIPPIN':

Janaia had been watching the pretty, young lady all day because opportunity by no means gave her the chance to confront her victim up close. Janaia had nearly run out of patience. She wanted to say, "Fuck it" and confront her target in public. She was really tired of sitting in her car and walking all over the city following this rut of a woman who thought the world revolved around her. But Janaia also knew that she was smarter than a fifth grader and that patience is a virtue and had been her close companion for years.

Observing the young, pretty woman for five hours straight was smoldering Janaia up inside. Finally she saw a window of opportunity.

Cool's girl, Cinnamon, was a pretty little thing that stood 5'4" and favored a young, Lisa Raye. She always stayed fly with all the latest threads you could imagine. I mean, she had to have it all–Chanel, Gucci, Dolce and Gabbana, Jimmy Choo, and whatever other labels that would cost a nigga a foot and an arm to get. Cool took real good care of his girl. He always made sure that she was in the limelight of the city's best bars and clubs to flaunt the expensive gifts he bought her. Yet, when he went down river for another dope case, she kicked him hard in the balls by fucking around on him with some jerk chicken-eating-ass Jamaican. Now, it was time for Cinnamon to pay for Cool's death with her own young life.

Hoping to bring this chase to an end, Janaia continued to watch Cinnamon as she made her way towards the Dillard's store at Beachwood Mall. The air-conditioned atmosphere brought small goose bumps to Janaia's arms as she followed ten to fifteen feet behind Cinnamon.

Cinnamon stopped to look at some jeans. Janaia made sure to keep a close eye on her. Cinnamon grabbed four pairs of denims and marched towards the dressing area. With her palms beginning to sweat from the excitement she was now feeling, Janaia also grabbed an armful and headed towards the dressing area. Before entering her own little cubicle, Janaia looked under the rest of the cubicles to make sure no other women were in there.

The devil had to be on Janaia's side because there was not one single soul in the dressing room with them to prevent her from doing her devilish sins. Janaia slid into the booth next to Cinnamon and tossed the jeans on the small bench. She then pulled out some plastic gloves and a plastic bag from her purse and placed them on top of the jeans. Janaia then pulled out the P-89 Ruger with the silencer and cocked it. Grabbing what she needed, she then walked out of her booth and knocked politely on Cinnamon's door.

Cinnamon called out, "Who is it?"

Janaia replied, "It's the manager. I'd like to have a word with you, please."

Cinnamon stepped to the door wearing a pair of black lace panties. "What can…?" Before Cinnamon could utter one more vowel, she was looking down the barrel pointed right in her pretty yellow face.

Janaia said, "Bitch, you scream and I'll splash your thoughts up on that wall. Now back the fuck up into the booth."

Knowing the scared Cinnamon would listen to her every

command; Janaia walked in and locked the door behind them both. Cinnamon was crying and asking what was all this about and what was going on. "Bitch, this is a message from Cool and his boys."

Cinnamon's heart could've busted in her small chest. She tried to plead to Janaia, "I didn't do it. I swear I had no idea that it was going to go down," she cried. "Please believe me. I got a little girl to raise." Those were her last words. The quiet pop took off the top of Cinnamon's head pushing pieces of her expensive weave up against the cubicle walls and hangers.

Once Cinnamon's body hit the floor, Janaia quickly picked up her lifeless body and sat her on the small bench. Reaching inside her pants pocket, Janaia pulled out a shank and began to jab the sharp object into Cinnamon's pretty brown eye sockets. Janaia pushed and pulled 'til she seen Cinnamons eyeballs pop out and hang out her baffled and confused face. Slicing the few loose tendons and veins that sat attached to the eyeball, Janaia then placed them shits into the plastic bag. This was a vicious and ill job, but this is what Hectic asked of her and this is what she was going to do for him. After securing the plastic bag that contained the loose, brown eyeballs, Janaia then peeked back out from under the cubicles to make sure the coast was s clear. She cast one last look to make sure she had left no evidence. Then, Janaia walked out of the dressing room and the store as if there was no bargain that had caught her eye.

HECTIC:

I had just hung up the phone from talking to my boy up in New York. We ain't never did no business or no shit like that.

But we were in the process of seeing what could be done about that. Money needed to be made and I was willing to make it in basketfuls now since I was in the building.

Me and Dave was caking off the sting we hit on Marcus' ass. We were now in the position to do all the shot calling. All we needed was a nice connect and I think we might have us now if things went right once I went back up top to see what my nigga was hollering about. I just needed to concentrate on one hustle and that hustle was to push this work across the state. Busting heads and taking names wasn't our thang anymore—unless we just happened to stumble across a nigga snoozing.

I went back to doing what I was doing before I got on the phone and that was cooking. Now, don't get me wrong! I'm not saying that I'm like some gourmet chef a muthafucka be seeing on television. But I can do my thing in the kitchen. I had my spaghetti in the pot and the homemade sauce simmering in its pan. While I was preparing to get the meatballs seasoned up, my apartment bell buzzed. I rushed to the intercom with the meatballs in hand and pushed the button with my elbow. "Who is it?" I asked.

A female voice replied, "It's me, baby!" That was all that I needed to hear to buzz the door open down stairs.

I rushed back into the kitchen to finish my gourmet and waited for Janaia to come upstairs. I told her that I was going to cook up something special for us since we hadn't spent any time together in awhile. I could hear the door close over the water running on the sink as I washed my hands.

As I heard the heels click clacking on the hardwood floor,

I looked up. But it wasn't Janaia I saw. It was Jasmine's sexy ass standing in the middle of my living-room. She was standing in some red six-inch heels and a long grey mink coat that seemed to be out of place to me since it was hot outside. I was stuck for words and mesmerized by her beauty. Jasmine hadn't said a word. She let her body talk for her as she opened up her coat. OMG! Butt nakedness met my gaze. I was as dumbfounded as if I had seen Jesus himself. My mouth hung open like an airplane carrier.

Jasmine smiled lazily and purred, "Is that all you're going to do? Am I going to have to do this by myself?" I hurriedly—and I mean, hurriedly—walked over to this goddess of a woman and grabbed her by her hair forcefully as I stuck my tongue deep into her mouth.

The kiss was aggressive. Jasmine moaned to let me know I had taken control of the situation at hand. She pulled away from me, tearing my shirt off while licking my chest and stomach like a wild animal in heat.

I couldn't do nothing but shake and shiver like a child on a roller coaster ride. Chills and excitement raced through my veins like hollow tunnels to the under world. Not able to take the warm ticklish kisses she was putting over my body; I seductively pulled the mink coat off her luscious body and begin to kiss her on the top of her shoulders gently making my way towards her flawless round breasts. I could tell that she approved of this behavior because she placed her hand behind my head as if I was an infant in need of her motherly milk and love.

I had no time to spare. I forcefully spun her around and bent over the leather couch. I began to eat her pussy from behind. Her secret garden smelled of strawberries. She moaned and gyrated her love muscle up against my tongue. I knew from the heavy breathing that was escaping from her well-shaped body, that she was ready to explode. So, I continued my journey 'til she screamed out my name and exploded on my tongue and lips.

Feeling it to the fullest, Jasmine screamed for me to put this meat up in her. Without second-guessing it, you could believe I did just that. With a sigh, she lay back and grabbed both heels pulling her legs all the way back towards her ears. I hit it from the back and later she rode me like she was in the Kentucky Derby and I was her lucky horse named, 'Get Money'. That's exactly what I was doing--getting money. She came hard for the second time tonight.

When all the action was over with and we were letting our heated bodies cool off, Jasmine began to cry. She said, "I'm a straight up bitch that needs a straight up nigga. I need someone that is going to be real with me and love me how I love them."

I couldn't say shit as I lay on the floor next to her holding her close to me not wanting to let go. I wasn't that nigga who could keep it real with her.

CHAPTER *12*

SUKI:

Wintertime always came with a leaping right hook to the residents of the city of Cleveland. The breeze that came off of polluted Lake Erie was blistery to the flesh. It sent chills straight through my body French kissing the marrow in the muthafucka's bones. When it came to showering us with its freezing furry, it was never something pleasant to the soul. The winters would shut down the whole city and leave a nigga locked up in his own home nine times out of ten with someone a nigga didn't want to be in the company of.

Anyways, I wasn't just lying low in the house because of the strong winds that was tossing bodies around like rag dolls. I was lying low because word had got to me that the police was on the hunt for my black ass. It's been over three months since Dirty told me that the police had stormed Page a couple of times looking for a nigga. I mean, I was out in the streets doing so much gritty shit that I had no idea what they were looking for me for in the first place. Nevertheless, I did know this: I wasn't about to turn myself in to see what the fuck the problem was. Whatever it was, I'm pretty sure it was going to get a nigga locked up.

Damn! These past few months had been dreadful for the kid. I was too nervous to run around the city, knowing one of these ho ass muthafuckas would drop a dime on me for that two-thousand-dollar reward that I was sure was on my head. People out in the streets struggling right now and was definitely game to make some easy money. Shit! I was game to make some easy money, too, if I could. Not being able to get out there and get mine the way that I knew how, my money was now vanishing away like the green leaves on the trees that was now turning orange and red. My snorting habit was catching up to my ass with quickness. Niko had left me alone because my name was fucked up on the streets. Now don't get me wrong! I wasn't scared to get no money because if you've been reading my story, then you know how I already got down. I go stupid hard. But, times were really hard for me right now. I mean really fucked up.

I heard from the streets that Hectic and Dave was getting money now and had no reason to do stick ups anymore. If I could only get close enough to one of those niggas, I swear I would have no problem snatching out their souls like a dentist snatching out a rotten, dead tooth. Yeah! We all grew up together. All that sounded good. But, times were serious right now and by all means necessary, I needed to get back on top.

While sitting in the kitchen looking out the window smoking on a cigarette, I heard a police siren in the distance.

The sound forced me to grab the AK 47 that sat on the kitchen table next to a plate of chicken bones from the night before. Once I seen everything was acceptable and my damned heart rate had went back down to its normal pace, I walked slowly back into my bedroom shakin' my head in disgust. I couldn't believe where my life was headed at this moment and where I was at in my life just a few months ago. I was doing big shit and I was having my damned way. Now I was stuck in the house smoking on some bullshit-ass weed and snorting some bullshit-ass coke, broker than a muthafucka. SNIIIFFFF!

After snorting some of this garbage coke up my raw nose, I glanced over at the bed to see this white bitch sleeping up in my shit. I looked at her tanned behind hanging out from under the sheets and I instantly ripped off my boxers and tank top like the Hulk to join her. I couldn't even remember this bitch's name or where she came from. But, it was all good to me right now. Sliding into this bed is where I felt I had more control of my life. I say that for the simple reason that I had no control of my life outside this apartment. I had straight up lost control of everything. However, I was going to shine again and I was willing to do whatever to make it happen again. Anything!

DAVE:

It was freezing outside but I had to get this snow and ice off my truck. Hectic had talked me into buying this Ram 1500 Quad and to be straightforward, I was feeling it. I ain't never been no truck man. But, since I had the money to blow like coke up a nigga's nose, I decided on getting it. Why not? I could afford it now without being broke at the end.

Me and Hectic had stopped smacking nigga's heads around months ago and went straight to fucking with the coke business. Hectic was trying to hook us up a connection in New York with some cats out of the Bronx. He was going to see if we could cop that white shit for cheap and bang it back here in Cleveland like a cheap porno whore starving for the dick.

In the process of us moving up like the Jefferson's and getting this bread, I met me a nice girl named Vivica. She was from West Philly. She had moved to the city to be closer to her ailing mother. Vivica had her head on straight and was trying to make something of her life just as I was. She was into the Afro-centric tradition and had that natural beauty glazing off her skin like a nigga's favorite glazed donut. I mean, this girl had me open like a Donald Goines urban book. I was tired of bed hopping with all these skank ho's. I was, in actuality, ready to settle down and build me a family. I had enough money now to open me up a small restaurant or store to continue to generate this money I was in control of without the police fucking with a black man trying to make it.

After scraping the ice off the windows of the truck, I ran back into the house to grab the duffle bag of money that I had to transport from point A to point B. As I got to the corner of Rawlings to make a quick turn, I spotted a woman standing on the corner who looked a lot like Jasmine. What the fuck was she doing on this side of town? Where was Hectic? Before I was able to rummage around for him, I seen these two Dodge Intrepids speeding towards me. "What the fuck?"

The snow tires that I had just strapped the truck with gripped the cold concrete like a nigga gripping a handful of ass. I wasn't about to allow these cops to snatch me off the streets after I was finally making a decision to change this lifestyle. They had me fucked all the way up.

One of the unmarked cars tried to ram me as I shot up the street trying to flee them. Nevertheless, the Intrepid was to damned light to be trying to push up on all this truck. "Bitch, step back" I yelled as I punched the gas some more, trying my hardest to speed away. I was now on Kinsman with a swarm of marked vehicles following behind me as if we we're playing some type of child tag game. The traffic wasn't that chunky because of the light morning rush. So, I had a straight shot to do whatever I felt I needed to do to get away from these damned pigs without putting lives in danger.

I spoke too damned quickly. I had to make a sudden swerve to the right to avoid hitting a cluster of kids either on their way to school, or trying to skip school. No matter the case, I was required to smack hard into a parked car. That didn't stop me from continuing to mash on the gas some more since the police was s on my heels.

Soaring up 79th like a damned maniac with no sense of direction, I decided to try my luck in the Garden Valley Projects on foot. I pushed hard on the brakes, forcing the truck to slide to the left and right. I could hear car horns blaring in anger because of my wicked and risky driving. Jumping out of the still-running truck, I sprinted between some buildings and an open field with a gun in one hand and a duffle bag in the other. I could hear the police cars in all directions screeching their tires on the black, cold asphalt as I attempted to put some distance between me and them. I tried my hardest to hide anywhere a dark space would allow for me to do. But, there was too many people looking out their windows being nosey as hell like black folks always are. I wanted to turn back around and go back the way I came. But I was stopped cold by a CMHA police officer. The old black man had pulled out his little police-issue gun, while ordering me to freeze where I was.

I could tell that the old black man was frightened to death because he couldn't embrace the gun steady in his wrinkled, old hands even if it was glued to his palms. I knew the old man had a family or a bottle of liquor that he wished he was in front of at this moment. I knew he didn't want to be a part of this .50 caliber I had in my hands. Yet I had no time to chat with the older gentleman and if circumstances would've been a little different, I would've given him an ultimatum. However, shit just wasn't going right for him or for me at this split second. My mind was made up on what to do. Wasn't any room for mistakes and right now the stakes was at an all-time high. POW! I lifted my arm so fast the officer had no idea that part of his brains was lying next to an empty potato chip bag and a small child's toy in the slushy snow.

I knew the police would be rushing fast to the area where they had heard the gun shot. So, I took my chances with the first apartment I ran up to. I twisted the door knob, opened it up, and then shut that bitch as quick as I had opened it. Then, I pressed my ear close to the door to hear if they had any idea where I had vanished to. I couldn't just give up. I was all the way in right now. I was knee-deep in some shit for the simple reason that I had just killed a police officer. Even though the old man was a housing police officer, he's was the fuckin' law.

As I sat tight to the door, a quick movement behind me startled me. I spun around, gun raised high, and ready to blast anything I thought was out of the ordinary. Standing in the kitchen doorway was a young woman no older than twenty-five. She was holding a skillet of scrambled eggs in one hand while her other hand rested on her slender hips.

"Nigga, who the fuck is you and what the fuck…" Before she was able to keep running her fat-ass mouth, she noticed the heavy gun that rested in my now-sweaty hands. Then she decided to shut the fuck up. "OMG! Please don't hurt me, mister. I was …"

Moving my index finger close to my lips to slush the nervous woman, I then told her to come over by me. Speaking to her in a calm but urgent voice, I said, "I want you to look out the window and tell me what you see."

The slender woman whose hair looked like a dead rodent on top of her head nervously walked to the window and said, "There's a lot of police standing around looking at someone on the ground."

I grabbed her by the arm guiding her to the two-toned couch so I could talk to her about a business proposition.

"Who the fuck else in the house with you?"

The scared-to-death girl said with tears rushing down her long face, "My two kids and that's it. I promise you."

I looked in the kitchen to see two beautiful girls eating breakfast, not paying any attention to what was going on in the other room. Stepping back into the living-room I said, "I need to chill here for awhile and I'll pay you for your time. I just need for you to not get all stupid on me. Because I don't have the time, energy, or patience to be playing games with you. I will with no hesitation fuck you all the way up. Now, is there going to be any problems?"

The young girl shook her head no and said, "Just don't

rape me or hurt my kids. I'll do whatever you want."

I walked back to the window and peeked out the curtains to see the police s looking around at the buildings. I figured they already knew I was hiding up in one of the apartments, but couldn't figure out which one. Soon, they would be trying to check them. Shifting my attention back to the young girl, I said, "I'm not into raping women and I promise not to hurt you, long as you don't do nothing dumb."

Finally putting the gun up, I then told the young mother that her kids couldn't go to school. I knew that they were getting ready because both of the young girls heads were done and they were both dressed nicely. She jumped up explaining to me that if the kids didn't go to school someone from school would come to check up on them. She had just gotten her kids back from the state a couple of months ago because of an old drug habit she how had control of.

Damn! So that meant someone would be coming by the apartment and be talking to the police about checking on the two girls. Fuck! I told her to call the school and tell them that the kids were sick. But, she said she would have to go next door to use the neighbor's phone because hers fell in the toilet last night. "Are you fucking kidding me?" I said. I stood by the front door and thought about what to do. I knew that I had to make the right choice because if I made the wrong one, shit could get real ugly real quick.

"Okay! Check this out. Do they take the bus or do you have to drive them?" The mother said, "They take the bus. I take them to the corner on the other side of the projects. It won't take me long at all." I sat and thought for a minute then decided on letting her go. I couldn't afford to let the school come here looking for the two girls and on top of that bring the police, too. They were going to check to make sure that I wasn't keeping the family hostage up this bitch. I knew how those cock suckers thought.

The young mother got her kids together and started to go out the front door. "Wait! Go out the back. I don't want you to go out the front where the girls could see something they shouldn't ever see." I walked her to the back where police was posted up heavy just as in the front.

"Okay, I'll be right back. I promise," she said.

I won't front. I thought about snuffing out this mophead bitch and her two kids and lounging in the house for a couple of days 'til shit blew over. Yeah! I know that was some monstrous shit to think about. But, I knew that I was taking a chance letting this bitch who didn't know shit about me give up my whereabouts. However, as far as I knew, I was already in a fucked up position and there was nothing this young girl could do to help me from the jam that I was in right now.

Right when the back door unbolted, the police turned around promptly and walked right towards her and the two children. I saw the pigs stop her and the kids to ask her something. But, the conversation was short and she was back to walking the kids to their destination. "That's good, baby. Don't say shit to them," I whispered to myself. Feeling a bit better about the choice that I just made by letting my only bargaining chip walk free, I placed the heavy metal on the table and called Hec. His voicemail picked up and I left a message for him to get at me ASAP.

Twenty minutes had slipped by and I was now getting a bit nervous. It didn't take no damned twenty minutes to walk some kids to a corner. I had the feeling that this hoodrat bitch snitched me out. Damn!

I ran up the stairs two at a time to the bedroom to take a look out the back window. The police had gotten thicker back there and was also pointing at the apartment. "Stanking ass bitch!" Knowing that the gig was now up, I ran back down the stairs, grabbing the duffel bag tossing the bitch upside down letting the contents fall to the floor. Pushing all the money to the side, I grabbed the AR-15 and the two clips and ran to the front window ready to act a damned fool. Noticing that no cops were anywhere in sight, I knew it was time to get it popping. They were sitting out there waiting for me to slip up so they could fuck me up.

While contemplating on my next move, I heard the bullhorn scream, "We know you're in the house. You need to give yourself up and end this right now." I sat on the couch and gave a small prayer hoping god could help me because I needed it worse than a muthafucka. I never thought I would be caught up in some shit like this. This thing I was in was far beyond my imagination. Now that I was in the focal point of this wild madness I had created, it was time for me to do what I knew I had to do. I checked the .50 Caliber and the AR-15 to make sure everything was ready and stood up.

The FBI and DEA was out there right along with the pussy-ass Cleveland Police. I kept a vest on for the lifestyle I was living and for the simple reason that the jack boys took no hostages in these wicked times—especially in these hard economic times that the whole country was under. I looked back out the window and seen a couple of officers running for cover. I pointed the AR-15 in their direction and started unloading.

POP, POP, POP….POP, POP. Pieces of bricks and concrete was busting in the air as I took dome shots at the officers trying to take cover. I then turned back around and ran back up the stairs to change my location on the officers who was huddled up in hiding.

The officers in the back hadn't taken cover yet. I caught some of them off guard. POP, POP, POP….POP, POP. I knew I had hit a few of them. Some were lying in the cold snow bleeding like the pigs that they were. I then ran back down the stairs. I had to hit the brakes because the officers were now shooting through the aluminum door and thin windows to the small apartment.

Silence had taken over the smoky apartment for about a minute or two. Everyone on both sides tried to gather their bearings. So, I grabbed my phone again and tried to call Hectic one more time. With no one still picking up, I decided to leave him a message. "Home boy, I'm caught up. I'm caught up so bad that ain't shit you or anybody else can do to save my black ass. Police are every damned where and I can't get away. Yo! Kiss my mother and watch out for Jasmine. Something real fishy about her and I think your girl the po…" I wasn't able to finish my eulogy because the police had kicked the bullet-riddled door right in. Nevertheless, they had no idea that I was standing right on the stair case looking down on their dumb asses.

As the police rushed in the door, waving their pistols around, I unleashed a nightmare on the first couple of them. POP, POP, POP. All you could hear was the bullets ripping between their suits and flesh as their pieced bodies began to drop in the doorway. Not caring anymore, I dropped the empty AR-15 and snatched out the .50 Caliber and starting busting that bitch as I charged the front door like a psychopath killer.

Leaping over the pair of dead officers to head outside, I was confronted by an officer who looked flabbergasted to see the barrel of a canon looking right back at him. With no hesitation, I pulled the trigger blowing an enormous hole in the officer's head. I ran past him before his soulless body hit the cold pavement in the courtyard. However, on my attempt to get away, I felt a sharp pain in my back. It slowed me down and forced me to piss on myself. Oh shit! My breath seemed to escape my body. Yet, I continued to burst my hammer like a madman. At that moment, all I was able to see was muzzle flashes. It was as if I was on the red carpet getting my picture taken by photographers from TMZ. I felt my skin being penetrated by small burning sensations. I continued to fire off my gun at any and everyone I could. When I turned around to try to run, I felt my knee give out. I looked down, puzzled. Where my kneecap once was at, was now a big gaping hole. Dark blood, muscles, and tissues poured from it. I fell to the freezing ground and knew this is where I was going to perish. Life as I once knew it was about to be over. I looked up at the clear sky above me. I watched as a collection of birds flew together, heading south for the winter and I wished I could be up there with them to escape this pain. Everything life had given to me from my childhood on Page to this dying day in the Garden Valley projects ran through my mind like old film. Blood was crawling out the corner of my mouth like a drenched bug. I smiled because I had chosen this life. This was the style that was going to take me out the game. My ticket had come and gone.I felt the painful sting to the top of my head. BLAM!

CHAPTER *13*

HECTIC:

I was in the Charger rolling heavy with a mission that needed to be handled. For the last couple of months, I had been looking for that Jamaican who had killed Cool. I thought he must have gotten away. Well, in my search, I had found out where the nigga, Dingo be hanging out at. I thought about paying his ass a little visit today. Now don't think for one minute that I had stopped looking for Suki or that traitor-ass bitch, Nikki. Shit wasn't lying like that. I was playing my hand like a Royal Flush because I knew, in due time, everything that rested in the dark always came to the light. Therefore, I was going to sit back and wait for that opportunity to illustrate its pretty face.

It was close to eight thirty in the morning. The restaurant might be a little crammed with its breakfast eaters and early workers. However, I didn't give two rats' asses about that. I owed this nigga and I was going to pay him in full. I know the fool got the message when I sent Cinnamon's eyeballs to him. I wrote on a piece of paper, "eyes are watching," to let him know that a nigga was watching his steps at all times. Now, it was my time to do what I promised Cool's mother I would do: Not let this nigga get away with killing her son.

When I hit 76th and Union, I pulled up front of the Jamaican eatery called, Big Pot. Once in front of the establishment, I killed the engine and reached in the backseat for the Mac-11. Cocking that muthafucka to life, I jumped out of the car and stuck the gun in my leather. I walked slowly inside the spot. I heard the chatter of a few early customers who were eating plates of Ackee, salt fish, yellow yams, dumplings, and green bananas, swallowing the tasty meal down with a cold glass of carrot juice while listening to the sounds of Peter Josh over the speakers. I seen old boy posted up in the back of the spot with a few of his island buddies by his side. They was laughing it up and having a helluva good time rocking they gold and ice and shit like Slick Rick the Ruler. Nevertheless, I was about to clear them niggas' nostrils out. I was about to hit 'em with the bionic.

Some Jamaican girl that was thicker than a pot of cold oatmeal came to take my order. "Wha can I getcha?"

I politely said, "Let me just get a glass of orange juice 'til I make up my mind. And can you show me where the men's restroom is at?"

"Yuh, mon. It's over der." She pointed me in the right direction that I needed to be going. Once she walked away, I stood up and walked towards the bathroom. It was in the back, next to the about-to-be-sleep island cats. While I made my way towards them, the three Jamaicans noticed me and stopped chatting. They were trying to rock me with their dogmatic grills. They had no effect on a bona fide dogmatic ass nigga as myself. It was all good straight up and down because they about to respect heat holders.

I turned into the small hallway and pulled out the Mac-11 not looking back. I was the muthafuckin' original rude boy now. Walking back into the eating area, I screamed out, "Eyes are watching!"

With that, Dingo looked my way, startled. Food dropped out his wide mouth when he seen me standing in the doorway toting the Mac that was ready to spit. Before I allowed for any of the blood clots to reach for their heat, I started busting like a nigga just got finish hitting some good pussy. I hit one of the island cats right in the head and neck. His blood spurted over Dingo and his other comrade who was now flipping over the table praying that the table could stop the fuming slugs from penetrating them. Screams, yells, and this Mac-11 filled the air up in the restaurant that I was about to shut down. Dingo, with no indecision, tossed his buddy out into the line of fire, demonstrating how much he treasured their camaraderie. I didn't give a damn. I lit his ass up like a Christmas tree. Every bullet touched his soul inward and outward, dropping his limp bloody body to the ceramic floor. Realizing that he had no more friends to throw to the wolves, Dingo tossed his hands up in the air, giving up. Oh shit! This was as easy as taking candy from a baby.

I dropped the Mac to the floor rushing the scared jerk-chicken-eating muthafucka. I snatched him by his nasty-ass dreads, punched him dead in his mouth a few times, then banged his face off the dirty floor 'til it split open like a watermelon. Then, I pulled him into the middle of the restaurant for everyone to see the blood-clot-ass nigga. He was crying and saying, "Whacha wont wit me, mon? I've done nothing to yuh." I calmly said, "Those pair of eyes I sent to you was from your girl, Cinnamon."

His eyes got big as manhole covers. He said, "Jah will getcha back for dis ding yuh do. Fuck yuh batty bouy." I looked down at the whimpering coward and said, " Fuck you and your Jah." Afterwards, I pulled an ice pick from my back pocket and jabbed Dingo right in his throat on top of his Adam's apple. The ice pick dug deep into his throat as he tried to squirm away from me. "Bitch, where you think you going?" I pulled the prison butcher out and jabbed him again, this time leaving the shank deep in his throat watching the bitch bleed to death. He reached for his throat with both hands trying to stop the bleeding but me and everyone else watching knew that wouldn't help. He was gagging and spitting up blood. I watched the nigga that killed my best friend die right in front of my eyes.

Satisfied with my work, I walked nonchalantly to the cash register and tossed two stacks I had wrapped in rubber bands on the counter to the old lady who watched in horror as I brung madness to her establishment.

SUKI:

I was exhausted and dead beat from sitting up in this apartment like a prisoner waiting on death row. I was looking forward to spreading my wings and letting my presence be felt on these soft-ass niggas in the streets who didn't believe in those ghost storied told to them when they were younger.

I flipped over the stained mattress and threw that bitch to the floor as I grabbed the long barrel .357 and the chrome sawed off shotgun. Making sure I had enough shells to chalk some bodies out with, I then made a call to Dirty and told that nigga it was time to get it popping. He knew what time it was and if he didn't, he'd better had act as if he did.

I had to put my Range on the market because I needed the money to support my ghetto fabulous lifestyle of fucking white ho's in the raw and snorting coke up my rough and ready nose. I had burnt up all my money like the inside of my nose while staying cooped up in this damned apartment, afraid to hit the boulevards, worried someone was going to rat me out to the police. As of today though, I didn't give a fuck and muthafuckas was going to pay with their lives for these empty pockets I now carried around with me like my own shadow.

While waiting for Dirty to come pick me up, I pulled out the little powder that I had left in my possession. I made me a few lines on a Chris Brown CD case that I should've thrown away days ago. SNIIIFFFF! Eww! Shit! This was the main reason that I had to go out and bust a few noggins. SNIIIFFFF!

Higher than a hot air balloon on a windy day, I heard a car horn blaring in the distance from down below. Peeking outside the window to make sure that it was Dirty and not some type of set up by the police, I felt a bit relieved to see a car that I recognized. I grabbed the gear that I would need on this evening and hurried my ass down the stairs to the running Honda Accord Dirty was pushing.

"What's the deal, my nigga?" he asked. I continued to look out the side view mirror 'til I was sure that we weren't being followed.

Then I said, "Yo, we got to make this move, Daddy. I got to get the fuck out of town and I need some money."

Dirty said, "What you got lined up?"

I looked the nigga up and down and said, "What the fuck you asking all these questions for? Just roll and you'll see. Damn!"

In return, Dirty didn't say shit the rest of the way to our target. Dirty was my boy and I had mad love for him. Shit! He grew up with Hectic, Dave, Cool and me. This nigga knew the game inside and out. At one time, he was shrewd with it, but he had a monkey on this back just as I did. Instead of snorting coke and going hard with white girls that looked similar to Pamela Anderson, he was smoking that embalming fluid on an everyday basis, and going hard with bitches that looked liked your favorite hoodrat slut. However, fuck this nigga and his habit on some real shit. Right now, it was about Suki and that's all I was thinking about. I was going to use whoever to get where I needed to be at. Anyone!

We finally made it to our destination. We sat outside the house as we prepared ourselves to venture inside the cozy warm home. Glancing over at Dirty, I peeped him out as he began to put a mask over his thin face. Confused, I asked, "What the fuck you putting that on for?"

Dirty stopped in mid-action and said, "So they won't see my damned face. Why you ask that?"

Snatching the mask from the top of his nappy head and flinging that shit in the backseat, I said," Ain't nobody going to be able to point us out, nigga. Ain't nobody going to be breathing when we leave this bitch. It ain't that type of party. You feel me?"

Bearing in mind that he understood what was going on;

we both decided it was time to pay some old friends a friendly visit.

I knocked on the door as gently as a Jehovah Witness would, trying to recruit new members. I waited for the door to be answered. Right on cue, the door opened up. Niko's white girl saw me standing on the front porch with a grin of deceit smudged over my face like soap. Karen had no idea that I was about to be the Freddy Kruger to all her nightmares. She was about to observe today. "Suki, how you doing, baby. I didn't know you were coming over. It's been a long time no see."

Fuck all this shit this white bitch was talking about. I yanked out the .357 and pushed Karen's dumb ass into the house as Dirty followed behind me. "If you have the courage to scream one word, I promise to put your brains up on that ceiling fan. Now try me.

Karen stood in place shaking like a pair of dice in a thirsty nigga's hands trying to seven or eleven as she pissed in her booty shorts. And that was the way that I had liked to see all my victim to be muthafuckas.

"Take your shirt off and hurry up," I ordered her.

Karen was crying and slobbering out her mouth while trying to do what I told her as fast as she could, never taking her big blue eyes off the big gun. "Dirty, grab her shirt and tie this bitch's mouth shut—and hurry up," I told him.

Dirty rushed over and did what I said as he squeezed one of her plump titties through her bra with a light giggle. As quietly as I could, I curled up my lips and said, "Nigga, what the fuck is wrong with you? We ain't got time for that wild shit you on. Get your shit together, man."

When Dirty got finished doing what I asked of him, I

spun Karen around and kicked her straight to the floor where life as she knew it was about to end. Karen was looking over her shoulder, trying to talk to me through the shirt and her sad sobs. I walked over to the couch grabbing one of the cushions placing it on top of her head. With no wavering, I placed the mouth of the .357 on the cushion and pulled the trigger one time splattering Karen's brains all over the floor. The fluffy cushion caught the vast overcharge from the small explosion.

Now it was time to get to the meat and potatoes of things and get to my true purpose for being up here. I walked quietly to the basement door and gave the knob a soft turn.

On my way down the stairs, I could hear Niko's voice as he said, "Karen, I told you to keep your ass upstairs. What the fuck you want? Is you…"

Before he was able to finish his sentence, his big fat mouth gaped when he got a good glimpse of me standing at the bottom of the stairs. Quickly surveying the area, I noticed that Niko and this half-breed yellow-looking-ass nigga was cutting and bagging dope up like me and Niko used to do plenty of times together. My mouth began to water as I seen all the merchandise in front of my face. I had to have all of it. Not half. Not a little bit. All of it. I wasn't about to play no games getting it.

Bold as hell, Niko had the nerve to say, "Nigga, you got to be out your rabbit-ass mind coming down here like this. And who the fuck is this with you?"

I looked over my shoulder at Dirty as if to say this nigga gots to be tripping. Twisting my face up in a knot, I raised the shotty up from the inside my coat and said, "Ho ass nigga! You know what the fuck this is. So don't act like you don't. Matter of fact, step the fuck back."

I saw the pretty-boy-ass nigga out my peripheral moving around too much. It made the killa feel uneasy to the point that I turned my frustration out towards him and fired. BOOM!

The hot shell elevated the trying¬-to-be-slick-ass nigga out of the fold-up chair he was squirming around in. The heated slug chewed into his face, shattering bones, muscles, and tissues, leaving half his face dissolved before hitting the concrete floor hard. Witnessing that this shit was real up in this bitch, Niko instantly plummeted to the floor pulling out his Glock .17 and firing off few rounds at anyone that he felt was going to case him bodily harm.

As smoke and sulfur filled the basement air, I pumped the shotgun and fired. BOOM! BOOM! I just missed his lucky ass. Niko rolled up next to the bar and fired a few more shots hitting Dirty in the stomach as he tried to run away from the flying screaming shells. POP! POP! POP! I heard Dirty hit the stiff concrete floor as I was concentrating more on catching Niko slipping.

BOOM! A big hole formed on the corner of the wooden bar as I tried to push him from behind the small hostelry. Not caring one bit for my own safety, I walked and continuously pumped and fired on the bar 'til I was up and close to see Niko peeking his huge face over the bar. With the last shell I had to my name, I caught Niko in the top of his skull, pushing his hairline and brain back simultaneously. As his lifeless body hit the floor, brain matter smacked the wall behind him.

Seeing that everyone was DOA, I quickly rushed the table and snatched up all the grams of cocaine shoving it all of it into the bag that I picked up off the floor. During my spree, some blood had covered some of the dope, but I didn't care one bit. If it was up to me, then there would be some pink dope hitting the streets for the fiends to smoke. After stuffing the grams into the bag, I ran over to the dryer and opened it up to retrieve the money I knew Niko kept stashed in there. There had to be about ten to fifteen stacks. Feeling better about the operation I had just put down, I called for Dirty to roll.

"Come on, nigga. Let's get up out of here before the police come."

As I was about to run up the stairs, I seen Dirty laying on the floor holding his stomach where I seen a mass of blood covering this trembling hands. "Suki, I'm fucked up, man. I don't feel good. I need to get to a hospital." He knew damned well that I couldn't take him to no damned hospital, especially none out here where he was at. There was no damned way that I was going to let this wet-head fuck up my move. I wasn't going to let him in on the little secret.

I put down the bag and walked over to him to give him a hand up. "Try to make it up the stairs while I grab this bag and I'll get you to a hospital." Dirty tried to take a few steps but just wasn't able to. The pain that he was feeling was unbearable with every step that he took. As he leaned on the stair railing bleeding to death, I walked up behind him snatching his ass in a chokehold raising him up off his feet. The little brawl and strength that he had left in his dying body wasn't enough to stop me from choking his ass out. "Go to sleep, nigga. Go ahead and go to sleep. Don't fight it." I kept applying more pressure to his throat as he slapped my arms. His efforts got softer with every stroke. In a few more seconds I felt all movements in his weak body stop including his breathing. Tossing his unresponsive body to the floor, I quickly rushed the bag and got the fuck out of dodge. I was back in business and I wasn't going to let these clowns hold me down. I've always been a crooked-ass nigga and I was going to remain a crooked-ass nigga 'til the day I died.

CHAPTER *14*

JASMINE:

It had been over three stunning, lengthy months since Anthony and I had really got serious about this relationship thing. This gorgeous hunk of a man was treating me like a queen should be treated by her king. I loved every minute of it. I mean, this man was showing me what it felt like to be loved and it felt sooo good. I couldn't wait to get my ass off work to rush right into his strong arms. I couldn't remember the last time I was feeling like this. It had been a very long time since I'd felt this way. I prayed that this feeling would never vanish from my peaceful world again. I was really thinking about living up here in Cleveland and transferring my job assignment up here. I still hadn't told Anthony what I did for a living. I didn't know how he would take it for the simple reason that I was lying to him. However, knowing that this man was loving me so strong and loving the way that I rode that dick like a jockey, I knew he wouldn't be mad too long with me.

However, last night something changed my world and tore my heart into a million pieces. How is this possible, I kept asking myself? This man that I was so in love with could not be the one that this young crazy man was speaking so flippantly about.

I was told to come to one of the interview rooms where they had someone in custody. He claimed to have some very valuable information for me about the Marcus. I rushed to see what this person had for me. I walked into the small dark room to see some unclean scary-looking black male sitting behind the table biting his grimy fingernails. I wasn't sure if this man could really help me. But, I had no serious leads in the case. Maybe this weirdo could give me something to work with.

The police said that they kept getting calls from neighbors about an outlandish stench coming from this young man's house. When they got there, to their surprise, the young man had a body wrapped up in clear plastic. It was propped up sitting in the living-room as if it was a part of the furniture. The officers claimed that the young man said it was his brother and that he had been killed in a robbery gone bad. He also claimed to be the one to have killed Marcus and that he had information on his accomplices. The only way he would give up the information on the other participants, was if they allowed him to get the one who killed his brother. Was this character serious? Was he really going to rat out his friends if we promised him we would allow him to play vigilante?

I tossed his file on the table and looked at him before asking him any questions. I was wondering if I was wasting my time with him. "So, you got information for us about the homicides that took place a few months ago on Marcus and his friends?"

Skeet looked up after pulling some skin from the corner of his index finger and said, "You're damned right I have some information. But I'm not telling you shit if I can't be released to go find the one who killed my brother."

Confused, I said, "You'll give me the ones that helped you kill all those people if I allow you to go play vigilante?"

The weirdo shook his head and went back to biting his nails as if this was no serious matter at all.

"Let me hear what you got, and then we'll see if we can make that happen for you," I said. I turned on the tape recorder and listened to this man for over an hour. I couldn't believe what I was hearing. I had to leave the interrogation room and go to the little girl's bathroom to shed tears with no one witnessing my pain and heartache. The man that I was crazy about was being implicated in a murder case that I was investigating—a murder case that I was going to have to bring him in over. A murder case that would get him the death penalty if he was found guilty. This could not be happening to me. This just couldn't be. After laying out pictures of the names he brought up, he picked each one out as I called. So, he did know the people and for him to pick out Anthony was devastating to me. It felts as if I had been stung by a thousand bees stinging me at one time.

Afterwards, warrants were issued on Dave and Anthony by the district attorney's office. There was nothing that I could do about it. I couldn't afford to tell these people that I was fucking this man to sleep damned near every night. I couldn't tell them that I was in love with the man they were calling an animal. What was I supposed to do? I tried calling him beforehand, knowing that I wasn't supposed to be doing that and if caught I could lose my job and my own damned freedom. Nevertheless, he was my man and I was still his woman.

I couldn't believe that Dave had gone out the way that he did. The first thing I thought about was Anthony. Was he this actual devil of a man he was being painted as? Was he going to go out the same way that Dave did? What was he going to do when I told him that I was the police and that I needed for him to turn himself in? On the other hand, should I give him the heads up and let him skip town while some others dealt with it? I was sworn in to serve and protect the citizens of America, wasn't I? I had so many questions going on that I couldn't take it.

SUKI:

My mind was made up to do whatever needed to be done. Right now, I was on the road to total destruction. Destruction was my top priority to those who appeared to me in any fashion. Fuck the police and the Feds because I wasn't about to put on nobody's jumpsuit and eat those processed meals for the rest of my life. Anybody that got in my way, and I mean anybody, I was going to serve him or her up a dish that wasn't going to be tasteful to his or her taste buds. Welcome to the real Hell's Kitchen, muthafuckas!

Since growing up on Page with my mother, I had always had it bad. I never knew what it meant to have it good. My father went to prison for murder when I was two years old. My oldest brother lost his life in a shootout up on St. Clair. My youngest sister was born with a learning disability. Therefore, there was no one to look out for Suki, but Suki himself. My mother was trying her hardest to stay strong for my sister and me. She worked super hard to be our sole provider. Once that crack cocaine had hit the streets, it was all bad after that. Almost everyone I looked up to was now turning out by the small white pebbles that were turning hardcore muthafuckas out. My mother started mingling with the wrong crowd and the next thing I knew, the state was trying to take me and my sister away from her.

My grandmother stepped in because she refused to let those white people take and do what they wanted with her grand babies. While my mother ran the streets, fucking and sucking, what she could to keep her smoking habit together, granny took full responsibility for my sister and me. Living with my granny in Maple Heights gave me a sense of stability and honor as I tried to get my life together. I was doing well in school and I had met some unique friends that were far different from the ones I had back in East Cleveland. Weren't no kids running around carrying hand pistols and brown bags of dope that I seen on any everyday basis on Page. It also felt good to be able to eat a hot decent meal and be able to sleep without the O jay playing loud outside my bedroom door keeping me awake.

However, my luck was so damned shitty! A few years later, my grandmother took her last breath and the state was back to take my sister and me into their world of the justice. They took my baby sister, those bastards! But, when it came to me, I ran into the arms of the waiting streets, those same streets that took many good black people under with its false love and false honor. Soon after that, it didn't take long for me to start getting high, drinking, carrying hammers, and sticking those shits in nigga's mouth taking their hard-earned possessions. The next thing I knew, I was out in the streets trying to make sense of life.

When I came up on all those dead presidents from that sting up in the Chi, I had, in reality, lost my entire damned mind. I mean, I flipped on my immediate family and even the niggas that I had grown up with and who showed me how to survive out here while showing me real love. Damn! I had turned into a total monster. I was now lost in total darkness. It was over with and there was no coming back. Right now, I didn't care if I died in the streets because I felt that was in my nearest future anyway. SNIIIFFFF!

CHAPTER *15*

HECTIC:

I hadn't heard from Dave all day. It was strange because we were supposed to meet up at Dave and Buster's to get ready to watch the Browns play the Steelers later today. It was now eleven. The game started at one and I ain't heard from him yet. Now that was a serious problem because he was a die-hard fan just as me and the thousands of other fans in the city were. We had planned this trip two weeks ago. I know he was just as hyped as I was. Maybe I had missed his phone call while I was fucking around on Union taking care of business.

I gave Dave's phone a ring. To my surprise, someone else picked up. The unfamiliar voice sounded like a white person with a 90210 accent. I hung up and called Dave's home phone. His girlfriend picked up, crying. I really couldn't hear her out as I would have liked to. But I did take notice of her saying something about the police. "Hectic, the police are over here and they trying to tell me that Dave is dead. They said he shot some policeman and he was wanted for drugs and murder. Please…" She couldn't talk because she was choking on tears and snot that got caught in her slender throat. "Hectic, please tell me this isn't true," she begged me.

I was stuck for words at first. Then, I said, trying to calm her nerves, "No, baby. It ain't true." I was going to get as much information from her as I could. She was crying hard but I could hear her through her sobs as she said, "They looking for evidence against him and his friends. That means you, doesn't it? That's where you two were getting all that money from isn't it?" Dave's girl started getting all hysterical and shit. I tried to calm the bitch down. I didn't want her to draw unwanted attention what with the police running around the house and watching her like I knew they were doing.

"Fuck you, Hectic. You ain't shit and you're the reason Dave is gone," she sobbed. She gave me a third-degree tongue lashing. I could hear someone in the background ask who she was talking. This gave me my cue that it was time to hang up now. Shit! How in the hell was the police on us like this? What the hell happened to Dave?

Riding past my apartment, I wanted to go grab some money and a few other things, but I chose not to. If this was true about Dave, then that meant the police was hip to me and was waiting for me to slip up. "Damn!"

Riding through downtown to get on the freeway and far away from my apartment, I finally decided to check my voice messages. I saw a few from Jasmine and a few from Dave. So I went straight for what Dave had to say. I couldn't believe what I was hearing. This couldn't be real. He said something about get at him ASAP. Then it sounded like gunshots in the background. Then, he said something about Jasmine that forced me to pull the car over to the side of the freeway. I replayed the message and heard him say to watch out for my girl. Was he trying to tell me that she was the police? It sure sounded like he was warning me about Jasmine. Oh, shit!

I couldn't believe what the hell had just taken place. It was hard for me to drive. My mind wasn't really on this eighteen-wheeler in front of me as I thought about how I might be sleeping with the enemy. Now, Dave had to be wrong! My phone rang. When I looked at it, I seen it was Jasmine. My heart began to beat as fast as a rabbit trying to get away from an owl. At first, I wasn't going to answer it. What if Dave's assumptions were right? Then again, maybe he wasn't trying to tell me that she was the police.

I picked up the phone and acted as if nothing was wrong. "What up?" Jasmine didn't sound too delighted to hear my voice like she usually was. That was a bad sign.

"Anthony, I really need to see you. We need to talk." I mashed on the gas some more 'til I was going about 65mph to get to my destination.

"What you want to talk about, baby? I'm on my way home now. What's on your mind?"

Jasmine didn't say shit for a few seconds. Then she said, "I really need to see you in person. It's urgent. Matter of fact, I'll be at your apartment waiting on you to arrive. Please hurry up, daddy." Before hanging up, Jasmine paused and said, "I love you."

I didn't say shit because right now I needed to see what was what. If I found out that she was the police, I swear I was going to put that bitch on ice like Vodka.

JASMINE:

That nigga wasn't on his way home and I knew it! I could feel it in the pit of my damned belly. I had that police sixth sense going. I knew that Anthony was on to me, and who I really was. I don't know how he knew, unless Dave called him and told him that he seen me earlier on his street.

Just in case, I grabbed a squad and drove to his high-rise to see if I could persuade him to come in quietly without any harm being caused to him or any of the other officers. I hated to do this to the man that I loved. But, he was a drug-dealing murderer and he needed to be locked up away from society with the rest of the monsters.

The high-rise was surrounded by the Cleveland Police Department. A few other agents and I ran up to his floor. We kicked in the door, praying things didn't go farther than this. It turned out to be a waste of time. Anthony wasn't nowhere in sight. Deep down in my heart and soul, I was happy he wasn't here. I checked around his apartment, hoping to find something that would exclude him from the roundup. But, after going through his property and finding over fifteen hundred grams of coke, ten pounds of marijuana, and over sixty thousand dollars, I knew that we had the right suspect. He had pictures of him and Dave, some other guys, plus photos of Dwayne Nelson, who was wanted for murder and attempted murder up in Chicago. He also had a few handguns in his bedroom and a few assault rifles in his living-room and bedroom closet. Didn't no average man that didn't run the streets keep these types of weapons around the house for nothing. This nigga was out of control and I needed to get him off the streets before he did something to someone else—or to himself.

Making it back to the station, I walked in full stride to Petro's office. "I want you to call my office in Washington and ask to bring Kovac up here. He is an old partner and friend and a specialist in this type of fieldwork. I really need him to help me with this."

Petro put down the giant, greasy sandwich he had been stuffing his face with and said around the food still in his wide mouth, "Before I even do anything. Hello Petro. How are you doing? I hope your day is going well. Well Jasmine, I'm doing acceptable besides the fact that the Mayor is all up my ass like a wild hair. Other than that, I'm just peachy." He said nothing else after that and went back to eating his sandwich.

Realizing where he was coming from, I walked over towards his desk and placed both hands down and said, "I'm sorry, Petro. I just want to solve this case and I'm ready to go get the ones who killed Marcus now that I have a witness. And I need Kovac to help me make this happen."

Petro stopped eating and said, "What? You think my officers up here ain't prepared for this type of crime solving? We get a murder or two a day up here and my office brings muthafuckas to justice. And who the hell is Kovac?"

Batting my eyes because I knew that he was going to send for him, I said, "Kovac is trained to take down these types of criminals. You see a few officers died this morning and I feel better with my life in his hands. So, could you please send for him? And I promise we will bring this case to a close."

Petro leaned back in his black leather chair and looked

at me, rubbing his three chins. "If you promise to bring this case to a close very soon and get the Mayor off my back, then I will do it."

Standing up with a smile, I said, "You have my word that we will bring these muthafuckas to justice."
Petro didn't say anything after that and went back to eating his calorie-packed sandwich.

Kovac was a big white man who stood 6'6" and weighed in at 260 plus. He had served a few tours over in Iraq and Afghanistan, trying to hunt down Bin Laden or any insurgents that was hostile to his company or our country. Coming back to the states brandishing many medals, he then became a homicide detective bringing hell to all the dope boys and gang bangers DC had to offer a white man who was born in Idaho. There wasn't a dope house, drug area, gang, or shower posse that could keep him from busting up in the spot taking names later. He was rough and tough as the best of them and this was what he lived for. This was his reason for waking up everyday. This was his reason for wearing a big smile across his face.

Later that day, I had got word from Petro that I was to go pick Kovac up at Hopkins International Airport in the morning. You could best believe that I would be there bright and early.

SUKI:

Time was running out for my impure flesh. My frail body began to shrivel. I was twenty-nine years old and should be built like a strong stallion. But, I looked and felt like a sick thirty-nine-year-old. The streets was eating me up. Still, I refused to stop snorting coke—even if the shit killed me. SNIIIFFFF!

I had over two thousand grams of coke in my possession right now. I needed to get rid of most of it so I could skip out of town as swiftly as possible. I had made a few calls to some of my out-of-town boys that I use to do business with before everything went sour for me. I hoped these old connects hadn't heard that the police was searching for me and decided to not fuck with the kid. Didn't nobody want to be messing around with a nigga on the run from the law--especially the ones that was out in the streets living just as dirty as me. Come to find out, my name wasn't contaminated yet down in Akron and it was best that I got down there as soon as possible.

I hit the undersized city in less than thirty minutes. I cruised at a snail's pace, turning down Thornton to look for my buyer. Dudes was posted up on the block doing what all niggas did while posting up on the block: Getting money or trying to take some money. I had niggas glancing at me, trying to figure out who I was and to see if I was a quick lick to come up on. Yet, if these corny-ass dudes knew what I knew, they would fear me. I was bad for their heath like a pack of Newport cigarettes.

Tired of pacing up the street wasting the little gas I had, I finally found the one that I was looking for pushing a bottle up to his face. I pumped the horn a couple of times. Giggles let the bottle down, squinting his eyes, trying to figure out who was causing all the ruckus. The dude was used to me pulling up in my Range banging something heavy out the speakers. But, now, I was pulling up in this Honda Accord with the muffler scraping across the concrete. Shit had changed drastically since the last time I had dropped him off those five hundred grams of coke! Right now, times were crucial. I had no time to be playing games with him or any other punk who wanted to front. I rolled down the window so he could recognize me. Giggle said, "Damn! I didn't know that was you, Suki." I gave him a half-hearted smile and told the homie, "Let's take a ride."

Giggles jumped in talking non-stop to me about some bullshit that I didn't care about as he directed me to the Spring Valley apartments. These were the same apartments where LeBron James lived before making it big in the NBA and before he bounced on the Cavaliers to take his talents to South Beach.

Pulling into the parking lot not turning the engine off, I said with concern, "You got the money?"
Giggles laughed and said, "You know I got the money, bro. Come on up and let's take care of this business."

I looked at him with apprehension. I rubbed my inner arm up against the Mac-11 I had stashed in the waist of my jeans, while grabbing the bag that contained the merchandise that got a nigga some prison time, or got a nigga's shit twisted like a pop bottle cap.

When we finally arrived at the apartment, I could smell the fried chicken being cooked and I could hear the lyrics of Biggie Smalls penetrating my eardrums. Walking into the living-room cautiously, I also saw two dudes sitting in chairs, playing some type of video game on a worn-out floor model television. Not worried about these clown-asses, I continued to roll because I was cocky and had no problem snapping on niggas and smacking the shit out them. I snatched stripes off their sleeves and I wasn't paying these weaklings no attention. I just wanted to get paid and bounce.

Giggles offered me a seat. But, I chose to stand and said once again with a little more emphasis, "Where the money at? I got to get back up to Cleveland, man."

Giggles walked over to where the two dudes was playing and touched one of them on the shoulder saying, "Go get that bag that's sitting on the bed for me."

I watched closely as the chubby nigga rose to his feet looking back over his shoulder at me strangely. Not being slow to the game I felt was trying to be played on me, I knew these cats had their eyes on me and my thirsty ass had just walked into damned trap.

I wasn't going to second-guess none of these vagabond-ass dudes. I smoothly reached for my joint. With the itchy finger on the trigger, I continued to watch the chubby kid walk towards the doorway on some super-dumb, slow shit. Trying to pivot on me with a chunky .44 bulldog in his hands, he found out that he wasn't fast enough. Slugs caught his ass. POP! POP! POP! The hungry slugs bit into the fat boy the same way he hit the hard floor, face first, breaking his nose and knocking out a few bad teeth. Not hesitating to let one of these niggas splatter my brains in Akron, I then swung the gun towards the other kid. He was now up from the game, trying to reach for something. I had no idea what it was or what it could be. But I wasn't going to give him a chance to splatter my shit up in here. POP! POP! POP! The bullets caught him in the legs and stomach area. Blood leaked over top of the game console.

Feeling the urge to destroy everyone in the house, I noticed a young female running into the living-room screaming, "What the fuck is going on up in here?" I spun the now-hot, smoking Mac .11 towards her. The girl instantly shut her big mouth because she now knew the answer to her question. Death was what was going on up in this bitch.

I pointed the Mac .11 at Giggles. The young girl stood in place too scared to move an inch. I said, "I respect ya gangster because this is how I get down. But you chose the wrong nigga tonight. You chose somebody that had nothing to lose. Where the money at, fool?"

Giggles sat on the worn couch, shakin' like a leaf. He said, "Suki I didn't…" Before he could say one more word, I pulled the trigger on the ravenous Mac, allowing the bullets to munch through the couch next to where he sat. Giggle's jumping and twitching body leaped and screamed, "It's in the bedroom closet. I swear to you. You can have it all."

Turning towards the young, black, traumatized girl, I told her, "Go get the bag and hurry the fuck up before I fuck your punk ass up too."

She rushed back from the bedroom with a bag in her hand. I then told her to sit on the couch next her coward-ass boyfriend. I looked inside the bag to see what looked to be close to twenty thousand wrapped in hundred bands. Reaching in the bag, I picked up one of the stacks and flashed through it to only notice that under the top layer of the hundred dollar bill was nothing but white paper. Oh, snap! This nigga was trying to play me all around the board like Monopoly. I laughed out loud so he could hear me but deep down inside I was crying. I was on the run and he wanted to play with my money, time, and patience like shit was sweet. Okay, I was about to boost the crime rate in Akron tonight.

I looked at the stack of paper money this nigga tried to get over on me and slung it hard at his face. All the paper money flew in the air as if I was making it rain up in a strip club. Without shilly-shallying, I unleashed a sequence of bullets on

Giggles' small frame. The sizzling slugs bore into his face and chest area leaving the couch a bloody mess. When I was done, I looked at the young girl who had blood and pieces of ripped flesh on her soft skin and thought about sending her ass to the other side too. But, I chose not to. Instead, I turned around madder than a muthafucka and walked out of the apartment. Just then, the fire alarm went off. The chicken was burning.

CHAPTER *16*

HECTIC:

I pulled up to Janaia's condo, which was way out in Rocky River. In this pleasant suburb, a nigga could find Porches, Benz's, and BMW being pushed by lawyers and surgeons that worked at the famous Cleveland Clinic. As for blacks living out here, the percentages was just as low as finding a white person living in East Cleveland. Very slim! Therefore, I prayed I didn't get pulled over by the racist police out here. I wasn't going to be talking; I was going to be letting the Mac speak. Point blank!

Before stepping out of the car, I gave the area a nice surveying, and then hurried up to Janaia's front door. I rang her doorbell and waited for her to greet me.

I finally heard a sexy female voice over the intercom saying, "Speak your issue."

I quickly said, "It's me, baby."

Within seconds, she opened the door to her beautiful

establishment. Janaia had a stunning home that fit her style. Real elegant and real simple to the touch. "Hey, baby. What's up with you and what brings you all the way out here, boy?" She was wearing some silk pajamas with a matching silk robe. It clung tightly to her well-shaped figure. I tried not to look because she was like my sister and I knew I had to keep the relationship just as that.

"I got some problems going on and I don't know what the fuck to do." I said.

She walked over and touched my face with her well-manicured fingernails and said, "I can see all the stress in your face. What's up, baby?"

I didn't drink but I asked her to grab me something strong from the bar in the dining-room. She came back with a bottle of Hennessey and watched me as I took a long swig straight from the bottle.

After allowing for the burn in my throat to disappear, I calmly said, "Dave's dead."

Rushing to stand in front of me, Janaia said, "What! What the hell are you talking about, Hec?"

I took another long swig, and then told her everything that had taken place this morning. Janaia was heated and wanted to go out and do something to Jasmine. But, I told her that wasn't the answer to my problems. I just wanted to lie down for awhile to get my thoughts together. One way or another, this had to be handled. I wasn't going to be able to run from the law for the rest of my life.

She walked me to the guest room with tears in her eyes. "You took me off the streets when I had no one. You never disrespected me and I'll be damned if you have to go through this alone. We a crew and we're going to go down as a crew. I got your back just as you have mine." With that, she gave me a soft kiss on my lips and walked out of the room to leave me be.

The next morning, I awoke to my phone buzzing in my pocket. I saw that it was Jasmine. I refused for this bitch to be sweating me early in the morning as if she was shot calling. Instead, I got up and went and got in the shower as I always started my day. Coming out of the bathroom, I could smell the bacon and eggs coming from the kitchen. The sun shone through the clear, clean windows.

With a towel draped around my body, I walked into the kitchen to see Janaia standing over the hot stove. She was beautiful. I still didn't understand how she was single. "Good morning, baby."

Before I could speak, I saw a 30.6 sniper's rifle sitting on the couch next to the case that it had come in. It contained a giant scope and a silencer to ease the noise of the powerful weapon on the tip of the muzzle. Janaia caught a glimpse of what I was looking at and said nonchalantly, "You know how I get down and ain't nothing else to talk about. I'm going to make sure that you're okay. Now do you want to eat or not?"

I couldn't say shit because she always had my back just as I had hers. Cool and Dave was now dead, and Suki was a lost soul. Righteously, I had no one in my corner but her. So, 'til Jasmine decided on calling back—which I knew she would—I'd go ahead and smash this breakfast that smelled so good.

JASMINE:

It was freezing outside. Yet the sun was out in full bloom

shining on a winter scene that would make any painter go to canvas. I was really happy to be meeting Kovac this morning. It had been a few months since I'd seen him. I felt a little bit more comfortable now that he would be here with me.

I tried to call Anthony this morning, but I didn't get through to him. I was going to call him back and I hoped that he would pick up this time. I couldn't get one wink of sleep last night because it was so hard for me to believe that the man I was in love with was a total opposite to what I had thought. I tried and tried to convince myself that they had the wrong man. However, the photos I found and a witness that I spoke with put him at the murder scene. All the evidence was pointing at him. There was nothing I could do about it.

In my daydreaming, I could hear the speaker scream, "Flight 301 from Washington DC has arrived at gate 13." Getting myself together, I made my way towards the gate.

On my way, I was almost run over by some kids who were headed in the same direction. "I'm so sorry, ma'am. My kids are just so excited to see their mother. I hope you're okay." The older white gentleman was very polite and I told him that I was fine and that it was okay. Looking at the kids, I stood wondering when I would have any children. I had pictured having some with Anthony. But all that had changed like the seasons. No one knew how much I cared for him. Now I wondered if he truly felt the same for me or if that was a lie, too.

Walking past the two kids hugging their mother, I had spied this huge frame coming through the tunnel towering over the other passengers. A big smile spilled over his face and I could tell that the giant was happy to see me. Kovac wasn't no handsome man that the girls would flock to. However, his personality made up for all that he was missing.

"Hey, little thing. How are you doing in up here in Cleveland?" I said nothing to the big man at all. I just walked up to him and gave him a hug. It had been so wild up here these last past couple of days that I just wanted to relax and go to sleep in his strong protective arms.

On the drive back to the office to introduce Kovac to Petro, I filled him in on the case and the suspect that was at large. There was no way in this world or any other that I would tell him that I was in love with the one we were looking for. Yet, in my defense, I never knew Anthony was the person that he turned out to be..

Reaching in the back to retrieve his bag, Kovac unzipped it and said, "Look what I bought."

I was trying to keep my eyes on the road and the massive instrument in his hands. I said, "Where did you get that at?" He was holding a gold Desert Eagle in his massive hands saying, "You don't need to know where I got it at. All you need to know is that this will knock a muthafucka back in his mother's womb." He started laughing loud and wildly as we got closer to downtown. I was so damned happy that he was here with me.

While Kovac was singing the lyrics to "Thriller" from the legendary Michael Jackson, I called Anthony's phone again. I won't lie. My heart started beating fast as I heard the phone pick up. He made me feel like a little bitty girl when I heard his voice. Damn! I loved him. We decided to meet up at a food eatery up in Cleveland Heights later today. He sounded real confident, like he did all the time. Once I hung up, I took a deep breath, and let all the impurities I had inside of me out slowly. It was on.

HECTIC:

I sat in the back of the taxi trying to relax and get my thoughts together. Was I doing the right thing meeting up with the woman that I was in loved but uncertain about? My thoughts had been going a thousand mph about Jasmine. How could she be the police? I knew that this couldn't be. If it was, I had no idea how I was going to react to the horrific information.

Jasmine knew about all the vehicles I had pushed around the city, so I chose to travel in a taxi just in case I was being observed by a number of police in unmarked cars and trucks. Before the taxi driver had the opportunity to turn up into the parking lot of Severance Circle, I had told him to stop. Hitting the brakes hard forced the driver behind us to hit his brakes too. He blew his horn and pumped his fist to show his anger. Before leaping out of the car into the chilly weather, I tossed the driver a hundred dollar bill and slammed the door.

Drawing the collar of my jacket close to my chin to keep the cold wind from traveling down my neck, I looked for anyone that I suspected to be the police. I strolled into the IHOP eatery that was crammed with starving customers. Shaking the rain and snow off my leather jacket, I saw Jasmine sitting alone in a booth. She looked as gorgeous as the day I had first laid eyes on her. Jasmine was a very dazzling woman, but she was going to be a dazzling dead bitch if I found out that she was the police. Real talk!

Marching towards the booth, I nervously looked around the jam-packed restaurant trying to see who was watching me. I couldn't see anything out of the ordinary. Jasmine stood up to greet me as if she hadn't seen me in years. "Baby, I really missed you," she purred. "I'm so glad that you came to see me." She reached to give me a hug but it wasn't as heartfelt as it had been in the past. I sat down looking to my right and left to make out where the exit door was located just in case shit got thick up in here and I needed to take a swift get-away route.

Feeling that I had all my ducks lined up, I then looked Jazz in her appealing brown eyes and said, "You got something you want to tell me?"

Jasmine sat in the booth across from me looking puzzled in a way I never seen her look before. I could tell that she wanted to tell me something but I don't think she was going to let the cat out the bag. Please don't let it be what my mind was tying to tell me. Please don't let it be that, I prayed.

"Antony, I have no idea what you're talking about." She tried to reach for my hand but I pulled it away slowly really wanting deep down inside for her to touch me all over.

"Jasmine, quit playing these games with me. Are you the damned police?" Jasmine's body stiffened. She scooted back in her seat saying, "Anthony, I love you and my feelings for you are genuine." Tears began to travel down her striking face as she continued on, "I don't want you to die in the streets like Dave did. I don't want that. I swear I don't."

My heart felt like it had just been stabbed repeatedly with a butcher knife. OMG! I couldn't believe what the woman I was in love with had just whispered to me. I never once said shit about Dave dying and it was now a true fact to what was driving me crazy for the past couple of days. The bitch that I was in love with was the damned, "One time."

I bit down on my bottom lip, filled with hurt and rage, I looked to my left, then to my right to see who was watching me and the ill shit I was about to reveal for all the public to witness. Reaching inside my jacket, I pulled out the .45 for Jasmine and the world to take notice of. Jasmine's terrified eyes lit up like Christmas tree lights. She hugged the fake leather seats. I hated to have to do this to the woman that I loved so dearly but the bitch had to pay for her fraud.

To my surprise and hers, the gun didn't fire a shot. What the hell! I pulled the trigger one more time. The gun still wouldn't fire. "Fuck!" I said. Before I could figure out that the safety was still on, I seen some big-ass white chump running towards me. Not having enough time to cock, aim, and squeeze, I knew I had to take cover. The big white man had a .44 Desert Eagle pointed at me. BOOM! BOOM! All the customers ran screaming for cover. I did the same—not scream, but run.

Just as I ducked for cover, so did the big white man who was chasing me down. Shots were now being taken at him as he jumped and dove between two tables looking for cover. Plates, cups, and bodies were being tossed in the air as bullets screamed loud in the big white man's direction. With all the commotion, pedestrians running around nutty, I was now able to take the safety off the damned gun and take the shot I wanted earlier. But, Jasmine was nowhere in sight. Then, I heard someone scream, "Freeze." Damn! I got caught with my pants down to my ankles. Before I was able to react to the command, the undercover officer's body began to quiver and wobble. Blood began to trickle from between his thin pink lips. The huge bullet that Janaia smacked him took off the back of his head showering some customers with his splattered blood. Before the undercover officer's body had hit the ground, I started running towards the exit door. I knew that I had to get the fuck out before it was too late. But, before I was able to make it to the exit door, I seen that big white cop back up chasing me down jumping over tables and people trying to catch up to me again. Who the fuck was this character?

Before the white giant was able to catch up to me, he hit the ground hard, landing on broken plates, glasses, and eating utensils. Janaia had started taking aim in his direction. As she gave me the needed time that I was in search of, I finally made it back outside. A police car that was waiting on my black ass, with no time to be playing around, I fired at the car non-stop 'til I ran out of bullets and options. Looking around speculating what I was going to do next, I threw the gun at the car as if I was a quarterback throwing a pass to an open receiver. Then, I took off running towards Mayfield and Taylor to get away.

Running full speed, I could hear the sirens in the distance as I made the effort to get away from those who wanted to fuck me up if caught. I was breathing heavily and my damned chest felt like it was ready to cave in thanks to those blunts of Kush and Newport 100's I puffed on daily. Running between houses, I was now on Euclid Heights Boulevard trying to find a helping hand. Huffing and puffing like the big bad wolf, I spotted what looked like Janaia's Audi speeding down the street. Cold and shivering from the freezing air, I took my chances and ran into the middle of the street, flagging the car down.

Once I was in the warm car, I began to calm down. I blew on my freezing face and hands. "I'm so glad that I have you, girl."

Janaia smiled at me with that wonderful smile as she hit the gas in our attempt to get away. Turning down Monticello to hit East Cleveland, we both spotted an East Cleveland Police car at the bottom of the hill. We weren't sure what his arrangement was for chilling there, but we was about to find out. Janaia stopped the car at the top of the hill and said, "They probably got most of the streets shut down looking for you. Grab that M-16 in the backseat and act like you ain't trying to get caught." Before we crawled to the bottom of the hill, I grabbed the assault rifle and cocked it making sure this time that the safety was off. There was only one officer in the car. As we approached it, I felt extra superior about what I was going to do to this lame. "Hurry up and stop the car, girl." She mashed on the brakes, and I swiftly jumped out of the car, swinging the Mac-16 towards the police officer, pulling the trigger before he was able to react to the loud claps. The shots echoed between the streets and houses as the blistering bullets chewed into the officer's body. However, the shots brought us problems that we were trying to avoid. Another police car was making its way down the hill behind us.

Whirling, I lifted the rifle up and fired off a few shots hitting the police car's windshield and hood. I watched the officer lose control of his automobile and smash into a tree. I jumped back into the waiting car, and Janaia hit the gas running over the corpse of the officer. "Oops."

Within seconds, another police car was tailing us. Janaia swerved around a slow driving ass muthafucka in our way. I leaped into the backseat of the Audi shooting out the back window to take easier shots at the cops trying to cramp my style. Aiming for the tires like I seen on a couple of movies from my DVD collection worked. The bullet took out the front tires of the police car forcing it to ram the side of the concrete barrier and flip a few times. I screamed in delight to Janaia, "Oh shit! Did you see that?"

I was geared up to turn around and jump back into the front seat when the car did an unexpected change of direction tossing me to the floor hard. Making it off the floor of the speeding vehicle, I noticed that two more police cars were behind us. "Hectic, baby, the police are everywhere," she screamed. "I can't shake these muthafuckas." I could hear the hysteria in Janaia's voice. She dipped to the right and left almost running up on the sidewalk hitting a couple. Not saying a word, I turned back around and started shooting at the cars praying that we would make it to safe ground and not lose our lives today trying to get away.

"Hold on." That was the very last thing I heard from Janaia before I heard a loud boom. I looked up to see that Janaia had run over a spike strip an officer had tossed in front of us hoping it would slow down the heavy out-of-control automobile. But it didn't stop shit. My baby whipped the car to the right taking us down Superior hill towards Euclid on two back tires and two sparking front rims.

At the bottom of the hill was a shopping plaza that we both planned on turning into to take our chances getting away on foot. The thin ice and light snow covering the cold concrete made difficult for Janaia when she tried to hit the brakes to turn up into the tight parking lot. BAM! Janaia had lost control of the Audi. She rammed a Caravan occupied by an old woman so hard that it flung me into the front seat. Shaking off the hard thud, I looked in Janaia's direction to see if she was okay. The steering wheel and engine enclosed my baby's small frame! "Oh shit!" Thick dark blood ran out the corners of her pretty mouth. Tears ran down her tender face. I was lost for words. I couldn't believe my eyes.

Janaia whispered faintly, "Baby, run. Get away because there is nothing you can do to save me. Save yourself." She had tears racing down her face. Tears began to well in my eyes. She reached for her .9mm. I kissed her on the forehead, grabbed the .38 from off the floor, and leaped out of the car. Hundreds of people gaped at us. I could hear in the cold air the sound of a gun. BANG!

I continued to run, pushing away tears. I had lost my whole crew. There was no one left but me. What had happened to us?

CHAPTER *17*

SUKI:

I took a couple of stacks and bought a 1999 Mustang to take me to another city—away from the madness of Cleveland, Ohio. I had been riding for about a day and I felt that I was far enough away from Cleveland to be able to take a safe and reasonable break. My ass cheeks were numb from sitting in this damned seat for over twenty hours. My eyelids kept getting heavy, even after I snorted a few lines of coke. From the signs that I was passing by, I knew that I was in Tennessee and a few miles outside Nashville.

I noticed a small motel to the right of the highway, in Hendersonville, Tennessee. I decided to pull in and snatch up a room for the night so I could rest my tired body. The parking lot was packed with eighteen-wheelers, Winnebago's, and smaller trucks. Drivers were either trying to get some shuteye, something to eat, or something to fuck. I noticed all the females running to and from the truck as I found a parking spot.

Grabbing my bag and securing the .50 caliber in the waist of my jeans, I calmly made my way towards the office. It looked like a shack. Entering the fly-infected office, I noticed a little old white lady whose hair wasn't grey, but a 40-ounce yellow piss color. She seen me enter the office, but refused to say anything to me the whole time I stood there looking at the Barbara Bush look-a-like. Loudly, I asked, "Can I get a room for the night?"

The old, wrinkled, lady still hadn't said anything to me. Instead, she clutched a tablet for me to sign in. Then she said with a bit of repugnance in her voice, "Sixty-five dollars and we have no ice, no cable, and no room service." Stepping back because of the attitude she hit me with, plus the stench of her funky smelling breath.

I then said, "Damn! What do ya'll have up in this bitch?"

The old lady smiled showing the two teeth she had left in her rotten mouth and said, "Rooms."

After tossing the money to the old lady while twisting my face up at her, I made my way back into the parking lot watching handfuls of white females running around the parking lot glittered from head to toe and made up like China dolls doing what they did best. I was from the city but it didn't take long for me recognize the country hustle that was being ran in the gravel parking lot late at night.

I wanted to capture me a few of the white girls who I knew would do anything. But my body was tattered and right now I had nothing left in the gas tank. No coke or piece of ass was going to wake this tired body up. Moreover, the white girls looked ghastly and there was no telling what these white sluts had to share with a nigga on the STD side. Therefore, I walked to my room to get ready for tomorrow and to see how far this adventure would take me.

Unlocking the door, I couldn't believe how shabby the room looked and how bad it reeked. The mattress was lumpy. I shook my head in disgust. But, it didn't even matter to me because I just wanted to lie down and rest my exhausted body. Right now, I could sleep in a doghouse.

I took the .50 caliber and placed that baby on the aged nightstand that had two good legs and a stack of books to hold it up from tipping over. I took off my shoes, placed the bag of coke and money under the bed, and took my ass straight to sleep.

After a few hours of resting, I was awakened by something moving around outside my door. I leaped up to investigate the strange noise. Grabbing the hammer, I walked to the small window and moved the thin curtains slowly to the side. There was no one out there. But a small number of trucks idled with their engines running quietly. I walked back to the bed to finish getting some sleep.

I was awakened for a second time by a cold breeze blowing over my body. I knew I shouldn't be feeling a breeze. I opened my eyes slowly. There were two bodies standing in the room. "What the fuck." I reached for my gun. The gun was missing. I was in some serious muthafuckin' trouble.

The shadow that stood in the room said, "We been watching you for the past day and waited for you to rest so we could have this little chat."

I was wide-awake now and looking around the dark room for some type of weapon to protect myself. I said, "Who the fuck is you and what ya'll want with me?"

Both shadows began to laugh. One said, "You remember that little trip you took up to Chicago? Well, you got to answer for that shit that went down up there, playboy."

My heart began to beat so fast that I thought I was about to have a heart attack. I screamed, while swinging my legs out of the bed, "I don't know what the fuck ya'll talking 'bout. But I can say this: You got your information mixed up, partna." I hoped this would convince them that they had the wrong nigga. However, I knew that the lie hadn't convinced nobody because one of the men said, "We been waiting long enough. Let's get this shit over with and get back to the Chi. Get yo bitch ass up."

I'm not going to lie. I was scared to death. I knew I was about to die. Placing my hands out between me and the two shadows, I said, "Hold up! Hold up! I got enough money and dope up in this bitch to pay both of ya'll. Won't nobody know shit if ya'll was to let me go. You can tell whoever the job was done and I promise ya'll won't ever hear my name again." I had to try my luck to see if I could bargain with the hired killers because if I couldn't, then it was going to get bad for me.

One of the shadows said, "That does sound tempting. I won't lie to you. But there is one problem."

The smile I had on my face had faded like a pair of old blue jeans. As the nigga continued talking, I could see they were putting what seemed like gloves over their hands. "The nigga paying us, want your head in this here bag. Now, tell me how you going to solve that problem?"

I looked at the object hanging from the man's hand in the dark and jumped up fast out of bed running straight for the door. BAM!

Not being able to run directly though the door like the actors did in the movies, I felt something hit me in the back. It shot pain over my shoulder blades and the middle of my back. I growled with pain as I tried to get up from the floor. I felt something leathery up against my mouth knocking out a few good teeth from my now-bloodied mouth. I landed up against the wall and door on my side as I took another kick to my midsection causing me to almost up chuck. I balled my sore body up like a kickball from the pain. The last blow I couldn't do nothing but rest my face up on the nasty, infected carpet. Everything went black.

Even though I wasn't fully conscious, I felt the bag going over my head. I couldn't do shit about it since my hands were tied. I sat feeling nauseous in total darkness. It was a fucked up feeling sitting motionless knowing that your ass was about to give up the ghost.

"Come on, bitch! If you going to kill me, I ain't scared to die. Fuck you Chicago fag-asses." I was going to go out of the game like a gangster. But that didn't do shit to stop the tears from rushing down my face. For once in my shitty life, I felt all the bad and wrong I done in the streets wasn't worth what was about to happen to me. Not even two seconds after I said that dumb ass shit, I felt a solid pain to the left side of my head. CRACK! I instantly hit the floor. It felt like the whole side of my head was missing. I couldn't feel that side of my face at all. I had bitten a hole in my tongue. Another hit came down on my skull. The pain was so horrific that I shitted on myself. Next they broke a few fingers. The throbbing sensation shot down my arm forcing me to yell out.

Knowing I was about to die, something deep in my soul

forced me to jump straight up off the floor to try get away. But the most recent hit from the aluminum bat bounced me off the wall straight back to the stained floor. I could feel the life escaping my body.

GINA:

I met a balling-ass nigga from 131st and Dove. He was getting that blood money for real. I mean, this crispy black Flava Flav looking muthafucka was more thugged than I've ever seen—and I seen a lot in my lifetime. And guess what? Then it came to me. He was really feeling me and I was feeling him too, long as he kept doing what he was supposed to do to make sure me and Jordan was taken care of. What you thought?

In any case, me and Ty had been messing around for the past four months and this nigga was talking about wifing a bitch up and everything. I stayed pumping this juicy pussy on his ass like a Chevy stayed pumping unleaded gas in its tank. I had him sprung to the point that he couldn't think about another bitch but me and that was the way it was supposed to be done. I had to make sure that I was doing my job right to keep this nigga out of another bitch face because let the truth be told, I would beat a ho down for trying to take food out of my son's mouth. What!

Ty had his business in order, owned his own home in Warrensville, had a corner store on Union, and wanted to open up a hair salon for me if I wanted to get into that type of business. He wanted to hustle just as he did and that was cool with me. I couldn't do hair. But I sure the fuck could find some bitches from down my way that did. I understood that my baby just wanted me to make something out of my life and I ain't ever had a man care for me like that. Damn! He was so sweet. It appeared since I stopped fucking around with Jasmine's funny hating ass, I was now seeing what my purpose in life was about. I found me a good man to take care of me, Jordan, and my fabulous needs. Huh! The same purpose I had weeks, months, and years ago.

My mother was doing well. She had stopped drinking and was now a full-time member of her neighborhood church. I was very proud of her for turning her life around for the better. But now she was trying to change mine like Dr. Phil. My mother was telling me to leave these nothing ass street niggas alone because they were nothing but trouble. However, I kept telling her that Ty was different and that he wasn't into that street life anymore because he loved me. So I thought…

"Relax, baby. I got this." I wasn't going to say shit to the police anyways. I wasn't the one driving and I had nothing to worry about and I hoped he didn't either.

"Okay, baby." I pulled down the visor to look at the beautiful person looking back into the mirror. I made sure that my makeup was on right and that I had no lipstick on my teeth before the officer in his tight uniform pulled up to the car. I couldn't help it.

The black officer didn't say nothing but, "License and registration, please." Ty reached inside his jeans and pulled out his license, then reached into the glove box and grabbed his registration, handing it to the officer who resembled Martin Lawrence, but a little taller. As the officer walked back to his patrol car, Ty seemed a little jumpy. He kept moving around and looking through the back window to see what the officer was doing.

"Baby, what's the matter?" I asked him. Ty said nothing as he reached under his seat and pulled out a brown bag, handing it to me.

"Gina, put this in your purse." I wasn't feeling this shit at all. I won't lie to you. But this man that I thought loved me said that everything would be fine and I had nothing to worry about and to trust him. And my dumb ass believed every word he said.

A few minutes later, another patrol car pulled up in front of us. Two white officer's looked ready in engage in some type of confliction. The way Ty started squirming around in his seat, I could tell that he was getting more nervous and so was I. All that, "everything will be fine" shit was a lie. When the officer came back to the car and asked for Ty to step out, Ty did, but he took off running in the opposite direction with the black officer chasing him.

Guns were drawn on me as if I was on the top ten most wanted criminal list. I swallowed my gum and I threw my hands in the air showing the officers I wasn't a threat. Oh shit! I still had this bag in my purse that Ty's bitch ass gave me. I didn't know what to do or say. If I spoke would the police shoot me? With all the police shootings going on in the city, I didn't know if that would've been a good idea. Before I could make up my mind, the smaller of the two white officers opened up my door and slung me out the car as if I just committed awful crime. It was on and I knew it.

"Get your hands in the air and don't you move. I swear, don't you move an inch."

I was so scared that I had no idea what to do so, I said, "I didn't do shit and he gave this to me." I tossed my Louie purse towards the officers and watched him give it to the other officer as he kept his gun and blue eyes on me. The bigger of the two white officers poured the contents of my purse out on top of the hood of the cruiser. My makeup, keys, more makeup and a box of rubbers hit the hood right after the brown bag had smacked the hood hard.

"What do we have here?" he said.

I shook my head and said, "I don't know. I told you, he gave it to me before he jumped out of the car and ran." After they unwrapped the paper as if it was a birthday gift, my mouth fell to the ground. A brown powdery substance wrapped in plastic fell out of the bag.

In my defense, I said, "I don't know what that is, but I know it's not mine."

Both officers weren't hearing none of that shit. They both rushed me and tossed me to the nasty ground fucking up my gear as they placed me under arrest. OMG! Are you fucking serious?

CHAPTER *18*

JASMINE:

I couldn't believe this black muthafucka tried to shoot me as if I was some stranger on the streets. I thought this man loved me. I knew Anthony would be mad and upset at me for keeping my occupation away from him and for lying to him. But, damn! I never thought for a second that he would raise a gun to my face and pull the trigger. Not once, but twice. And the look that he had in his eyes was not the man that I had fallen in love with. He was absolutely a stranger. I didn't like that look in his eyes.

Now this coward was back on the run again as a young woman he was with lay dead with the front of a car pressed up in her chest and her brains blown out on the dashboard next to a Bobbie Gibson bobble head that hadn't stopped bobbing back and forth since I arrived on the scene.

Anthony was a bitch. I couldn't wait to catch up to his

pathetic ass. I promised myself that I wouldn't be passive with him this trip. If he wanted to play gangster, then that's how we were gong to play when I seen him. There was no limit to what I would do to bring his ass in or to expire his existence on this earth like a carton of spoiled milk. Anthony was going to pay for his crimes. If I had anything to do with it, I would make sure that it happened.

Kovac came rushing up to the car as I sat in the driver's seat disgusted at what had happened today. "We got a hit that a carjacking was just committed a few blocks away from here on Fay. The description matches our boy. Come on! Let's get this muthafucka."

Rushing to close the door, I started the car up and placed the siren on the front dash, taking off before Kovac was fully in the car.

Before jumping out of Janaia's car, I had made sure to grab the .38 special that had been tossed to the floor like everything else in the ruined car. Panting, I ran down Wheeler to try to hit Eddy Road to get away. But police cars were everywhere. I knew it wouldn't be long before they located me on foot. Therefore, I had to change my plan up if I wanted a fair shake at getting away from these cock suckers. Right in front of my freezing nose and lips was an elderly lady sitting in the driver's seat of a new Chevy Cruze with the car still running. I couldn't believe how trouble-free this task would be yanking the older lady out the car without having to fuck her up. Running towards the car at top speed praying not to slip on the thin ice, I noticed a young man and woman walking towards the waiting car. I automatically cocked the hammer back as I quickly approached the vehicle.

The older lady must've seen me running up because I heard the door automatically lock as I approached the driver's window. Without saying one word or wasting one second, I smashed the window with the gun exploding pieces of glass all over the older woman. I quickly grabbed the older lady by the collar of her winter jacket and pulled her straight through the window tossing her old ass to the wet ground.

As I opened the door to get in the car, I heard, "Hey! What the fuck is wrong with you?" Looking towards the house, I saw the man running towards the car. I pointed the gun in his direction pulling the trigger blowing out the passenger's window. BOOM! I missed my target but I still got the reaction that I was looking for. The man halted leaving me the fuck alone and getting out my muthafuckin' way.

As the man and woman dove to the snowy yard to escape the hot slug I had fired at them, I sped off almost running over the older woman still lying in the street. My bad!

HECTIC:

I didn't get a chance to put the car in drive before noticing a speedy Chrysler Sebring flying down the street towards me. I knew it was the police before I seen the siren on the dashboard flicking red and blue. "Damn!" I muttered, mashing down on the gas pedal so hard I thought my foot was going to go through the floorboard and hit the ground. With the tires spinning hungrily on the asphalt and burnt rubber filling the cold air, I put the gearshift in drive.

Soaring down the street, I hit the brakes firmly and watched the car fishtail to the right, as I turned left onto Emily almost hitting an empty Salvation Army bus. Not paying attention to my surroundings and where I was going, my dumb ass had turned right in front of three police cars. They were headed up Emily towards me. I couldn't reduce speed to get around the cars as the police cars were fast approaching.

As the engine in the Chevy revved loudly in my approach to see who had the balls to participate in a friendly game of chicken, I saw the police cars veer off rapidly to get out my way. I felt relieved that neither of the officers had the guts to watch the heavy automobiles clash. Releasing my butt cheeks and catching my breath, I continued to fly towards Superior in my efforts to flee. Looking in the rearview, I became aware of the police cars hitting their brakes in their attempt to catch back up to me and not run into the Sebring that was still behind me. Not paying attention to what was in front of me; I couldn't hit the brakes fast enough. I plunged into the side of a bridge and hit a rider on his Ninja motorcycle. BLAM!

The impact smacked my head hard. The airbag exploded out the steering wheel fast. I hit the rider on the bike. It was wedged between the grill of the Chevy and the concrete bridge. The rider's legs and pelvis bone were crushed on impact. I shook my head and jumped out the wrecked car. The traffic jam stopped the Sebring from catching up to me. My head was bleeding heavily. The motorcycle rider was screaming. I looked around hysterically trying to figure out which way to run. Bystanders gazed at me in bewilderment. I could run up Superior or under the bridge to the Rapid station where I heard the train above me pulling up to the station. Fuck it! Clutching the .38 in my hand, I took off running between cars tooting their horns. I jumped and leaped on hoods and rooftops of vehicles to make my escape faster. I noticed that same big white cop now out the Sebring, chasing me.

The big white cop was faster than I thought. I watched his ass getting closer with every big step he ran. Ah, hell! I had something to slow this big muthafucka down. I fired the .38 in his direction and watched his big ass duck for cover. BOOM! BOOM! This slowed the super cop down some. I turned towards the Rapid station running as fast as I could to catch the train before it took off.

Entering the station, I took the stairs two at a time, trying to make it to the platform before being caught by the police or left behind by the train. But, before I could make it to the top, I missed one of the steps and fell hard losing the .38. I watched it tumble back down the stairs. "Shit!" I thought about going back to retrieve but changed my mind. I got my ass back up and began to climb the stairs. While pushing some youngsters out of my way, I heard a familiar sound echo through the staircase.

"Freeze!" There was no way in this world or any other that I was going to give in to that demand. I would die and go to hell before I did that. BOOM! I heard the bullet whiz past me. It shattered the glass door in front of me. Straight away, I ducked and pulled the door open to the podium. I stepped on the shattered glass and headed towards the train.

I didn't want to enter the train and let the big white cop trap me up in there, so I grabbed a plastic garbage can and stood to the side, waiting for him to step from behind the windowless door. I watched the passengers on the train looking out the windows towards me and hoped they wouldn't give away my hidey-hole. Right now, I was in a losing position. I needed a break. Snapping my focus back, I heard a footstep crushing the shattered glass. I swung the plastic garbage can in that direction. BLAM!

The garbage can caught the big white officer off guard. He was smacked dizzy. Seeing that the .44 had flown out his hands and landed towards the train, I quickly rushed him feeling my chances of winning this fight were just as good as his.

We scuffled on the cold platform like two wrestlers on a mat. I bit the officer in his gigantic face. With a portion of his fleshy face in my mouth, I punched him a few times in the eye before he flipped me over to my side, getting up before I could. Angry about the chunk of meat I took from his face, the big cop kicked me in the ribs, forcing me to spit out the bloody flesh. I reached for my ribs in pain as he tried to kick me again. I grabbed his leg and pulled him back down onto the platform, hurrying to get on top of him to smash his head hard into the concrete. After a few bashings of his head to the stained ground, the hurting big cop flipped me over his head almost making me fall off the platform.

Before I could get up, I was in the air crashing hard to the concrete. I banged the side of my head and face on the platform. Before I was able to get my wits back together, I found myself in the air again being slammed on top of the garbage can I had hit him with. BAM! "Oh shit!" The wind was knocked out of my body. I eyed the gigantic gun lying next to the train.

I tried to stop the cop from slamming the shit out of me once again. But, I just wasn't strong enough. He tossed me hard against the train almost throwing me through the window. I was in excruciating pain. I swear I couldn't take one more slam. "Yeah, you thought you could fuck with me, boy?" he growled. "I'm going to make you say my name before we leave off this muthafucka today," he hissed.

The gun was just a few feet away from me. The white giant snatched my ass up in the air again. Reaching with every inch of my 5'10" frame, I grabbed the pistol before being lifted in the air. I placed the muzzle of the gun on top of his head and pulled the trigger. BOOM!

One bullet from the .44 Dessert Eagle tore off the top of his big head. It continued to travel through his body, blowing a gigantic exit hole in his neck. Me and his dead body hit the ground with a loud thud. I was tired and covered with sweat and blood. But, I knew that I had to get up because I could hear someone running up the stairs to the now-bloody platform. I rose to my knees ready to try to get on the train. But it had already shut its doors. I looked towards the stairs to see Jasmine staring at me with sadness and hatred in her eyes.

JASMINE:

Before I could stop the car or get around the mountain of traffic that was in front of me, Kovac had already jumped out of the moving car to give chase. By the time I finally made it out of the car, I had to duck down behind a few cars to avoid the gun fire from farther up under the bridge. After the smoke had cleared, I began scampering in Kovac and Anthony's direction.

I couldn't believe I was pursuing the man that I had found so irresistible. This was the guy that I thought understood me, defined me, needed to hold me, and would stick by me no matter what. I thought I had found my everything in him. I trusted this man with my life and now he was pulling a gun on me! This black-ass traitor didn't give a fuck about my ass.

I made it into the Rapid station, gun drawn, ready to blast on sight. I saw a few people in the station standing around looking up the stairs that led to the platform. Before sprinting up the stairs, I noticed a .38 lying on the ceramic station floor. I scooped it up and placed it in the waist of my slacks as I was rushing up the stairs to aid in Anthony's capture, I was stopped cold by the roar of a single gunshot being released. BOOM! Squatting down to protect my own neck, I reached the doorway and stepped on crushed glass.

There lay my best friend, protector, and partner. Half his head was missing.

OMG! This couldn't be happening to me. Not the only friend I had in my life! The only person who ever treated me with respect and dignity, but also a man I looked at like a bigger brother. Please tell me that this was a bad dream. Lord, please tell me that this wasn't real. If I closed my eyes, then opened them, I knew I would be lying in my warm pajamas in my snuggly bed.

However, when I opened my eyes, the only thing that I saw was Anthony staring. This was my reality and shit was real. He was kneeling on the ground with blood and swollen knots painted all over his once-handsome, panic-stricken face. He looked like a furious famished lion that had escaped its cage and was on the prowl for fresh meat. Not one word had escaped Anthony's mouth. He rose slowly, looking at me with violence in his eyes.

With the glock .357 gripped in my hands, I said angrily

"Anthony! How could you? How could you do this to me? I loved you and you acted as if you ain't ever given a fuck about me."

He said nothing. I watched him closely watching me, waiting to see who was going to make that first move. Without warning, Anthony took off running towards me like a madman screaming words I couldn't understand. Before I could raise the gun to blow his shit lopsided, this fool was on top of me.

Snatching me up the hair, he slammed my face off the brick wall. I unconsciously dropped the gun that I had clenched in my right hands as the pain traveled through my small frame. I was dizzy from the nasty spill to my face. Anthony then reached back and punched me right in my nose breaking it on impact. CRACK!

Knowing that I couldn't afford to slip into total darkness, I fought to stay conscious. Gathering strength from some hidden source, I spun over and kicked Anthony square in his balls. I had learned that technique from a self-defense class that I had been forced to take for situations like this. My kick caused a little damage to Anthony. I then rolled over to my feet. As I rose, he tackled me, screaming, "Bitch, where you think you going?" Anthony punched me in the jaw not once, but twice. He then put his hands around my neck trying to choke the shit out of me.

"Anthony...Please...Please...Stop." I gasped, trying to hit him on the side of his head and face. My flailing hits were doing nothing to him but making him madder. He continued to put more pressure on my neck.

"I'm going to kill you, bitch. You lied to me and now you're going to pay with you life!" he shouted.

OMG! I could feel the life seeping from my body. I was getting weaker from the pressure he was applying. I could see stars. "Yeah bitch, die."

The punches I was now throwing was nothing more than swats on his back. He continued to slobber and spit in my face and talk a lot of obscenities. With all the strength I could muster, I reached up under my waistband to grab the .38 I suddenly remembered I had tucked away in my slack. Thank God!

"Yeah muthafucka," I thought to myself. I pulled the gun, cocking it. Hearing the hammer being pulled back, Anthony turned to his left to witness the small cannon. BAM! The muzzle flash chewed a nice hole in Anthony's side, pushing his wounded body off me. Wasting no time to allow this maniac to get back up to cause me any more harm, I rose to my feet choking and gasping for air, pointed the gun down at the man I once loved with all my heart. I pulled the trigger. BAM! BAM! BAM! I gave Anthony no opportunity to plead for his life. He had killed my partner and tried to choke the life out of me. I had no remorse as I watched the hot slugs tear through his flesh like a bear tearing through a fresh-caught salmon. "You live by the gun. You die by the gun you punk muthafucka," I muttered.

I tossed the gun to the platform and watched Anthony struggle to stay alive as police officers rushed up the stairs to the now-quiet and bloody platform. Anthony lay on the ground looking at me with those same eyes that I had once fallen in love with. Blood oozed from his mouth. He tried to speak. But, before I could kneel down to hear what he was trying to say, the life he once knew was over. The last breath of air in his lungs had escaped.

GINA:

I couldn't believe how crooked the legal system was! I was convicted and found guilty for possession of the drugs Ty's bitch-ass had given me to hold for him. Now I was placed into custody to serve eight muthafuckin' years I didn't do shit to get. How the hell could this happen to a bitch like me?

The state had placed me at the women's correction down on 30th. This was cool. I was still in the city and I could get the visits from my family and friends I needed to help me get through these ill times. However, it was hard to get used to this prison lifestyle that consisted of some muthafuckas telling me what to do, what to wear, what to eat, when to sleep, and shit. I was Gina, the damned diva of all divas! I wasn't about to settle for this bullshit. The food was horrible. I had no privacy, and I didn't like being around all these carpet-munching-ass bitches. Why did this have to happen to me?

The officer had just finished taking count to make sure that all prisoners was accounted for. I headed off to my rack and the restroom when they were done. I had to piss so bad that I thought I was about to die. Rushing into the bathroom, I hurried up and jumped on the toilet without even wiping to down first. Feeling relief as I drained myself, I noticed the door swing open. Two other inmates entered the bathroom.

Feeling much better now that I had an empty bladder, I wiped myself clean then walked to the sink to wash my hands. I had noticed the two girls in the bathroom giggling. But I had learned early to mind my own business. I knew they was about to get on some gay shit, so I knew it was time for me to go. Spinning to leave the girls to their business, I suddenly felt a hand on my shoulder. "What the fuck!"

Turning around to confront the bitch, I said, "Look, don't you ever put your hands on me. I ain't on that gay shit, boo." I wasn't about to accept no shit like that. If a butch bitch wanted to test me, then I was going to make my stand right here and now. The yellow girl with the mark going across her face laughed and said, "Bitch, don't nobody want your skanky ass." The other girl giggled at her friend's comment which I felt wasn't funny at all. The yellow girl continued on, "You don't remember me, do you?"

I took a step back to see if I remembered the bitch. She reminded me. "Yeah, you're the reason for this scar across my damned face, bitch."

Oh shit! I did remember the girl. We got into it at the gas station on 55th because she claimed I was fucking her man, which I was. The dude had money and he was paying for what he wanted—a piece of Gina. She lunged at me and pulled out the razorblade. Then she wants to jump bad with a bitch and pull down on me? "Fuck this bitch!" is what I was thinking before both bitches reached up their T-shirts to reveal the shanks they carried with them.

Panicking, I tried to run from the bathroom to get help from someone. I wasn't built for this type of shit. I thought she wanted to fight. Yet, I see it was on another level of the game that I wasn't ready for. As I tried to reach the door handle, I felt a sharp pain in the middle of my back. Before I was able to scream, my mouth was covered. I felt another sharp pain enter my chest. OMG! I was about to die in a fuckin' ladies' prison bathroom.

Blood soaked my nightgown as the two girls dragged me

into the shower area and continuously stabbed me. I couldn't feel the pain no more. I died in the showers next to two bloody shanks.

StreetLife PUBLISHERS

GET DOWN OR LAY DOWN

Warning: Read this with your lights on and your doors locked!!!

DERRICK JOHNSON

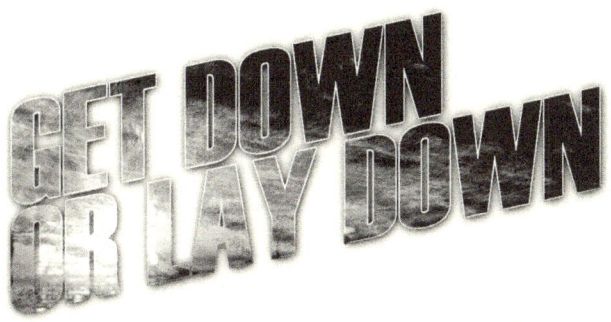

GET DOWN OR LAY DOWN

Quarter Man was sitting on the front porch for what seemed like hours waiting on the rest of the crew to arrive for their daily session when from inside of the house Dig a Hole yells for him to open the back door for the guys. Security was a must when it came to the gatherings, solely because they were the outlaws of the city and were notoriously known for laying niggas down and taking whatever, from whomever, they wanted.

At one point every member of the Bogus-D-Siples was once part of an organized gang ranging from GD, Vice Lords, Crips, and Bloods. One particular member of the gangs stood out, one who was different. He was extremely vicious and was always in disagreement with the laws and policies to which the gang was suppose to adhere. Never the one to accept the violations for his actions, he became looked upon as an outcast. Feeling as though the gangs never were originally from his city anyway, he secretly held the desire to rid the city of the outsiders, whom he considered to be leeches that were there to rape his city of its riches and take control of the streets he was raised on.

Patiently waiting for the right time paid off for Dig a Hole.

One day after one of the gang's meetings, he saw one of the head members take a huge bag and place it in the back of the trunk of his Mercedes. Not quite sure how the situation was going to play out, he knew this was his opportunity to make his move, and from this point on he was all in. Thinking fast he saw one of the shorty folks; one he knew kept a banger on him and was one of the many who were from Minneapolis who looked up to him and called him Uncle. He involuntarily involved shorty into his plot.

Laying in the cut like a bandaide, Dig a Hole instructed Quarter Man as to the part he was soon to play in the scheme. Patiently they waited on the chief Maurice to come back out of the building. Their wait wasn't long.

Dig a Hole knew that Maurice wouldn't be alarmed by Quarter Man's presence, mainly because at seventeen he weighed a buck twenty soaking wet with the looks of a twelve-year-old. But in his case looks were deceiving. This was a killa; a young cat with no heart or remorse for anything or anyone. He was abandoned at the age of eleven and was adopted by the streets, learning that success of his survival consisted of taking what you want. At eleven he was left at home with an empty refrigerator and a nine shot 22 automatic pistol he stole form one of his mother's many lovers. Filled with total bitterness and the will to survive, he left his home never to return, killing his first of many victims at the age of twelve.

Seeing the gangsta in him, Dig a Hole opened both his arms and houses to the young killer. It was an act of kindness that earned Quarter Man's loyalty for life to the man he now considered his only family.

Upon seeing Quarter Man, coming out Maurice hollered,

"What's up Shorty Folks?"

"Shit. Just waiting on my mans to come out," Quarter Man replied.

"Who's that?" Maurice asked, still heading towards his car.

Noticing Maurice not paying any attention to his surroundings, Dig a Hole emerged from the side of the building. Still talking to Quarter Man, Maurice opened his trunk. At this point Quarter Man pulled out the 40 Glock he had concealed in his waistband.

Speaking slowly, he told him to simply "get in the trunk."

Walking up to him, Dig a Hole saw a slight hesitation in Maurice's actions and immediately took control of the situation. He apprehended the pistol and smacked him upside the head saying, "Get the fuck in the trunk bitch."

Hesitating is what cost him his life. Not one to repeat himself, Dig a Hole put one in his head and watched him slump over into the trunk.

Looking back at Quarter Man he shouted, "Hurry up and stuff the rest of the body in the trunk." He almost gave him another dome shot when a nerve made Maurice's leg kick back outside the trunk. Quickly putting it back inside, they hurriedly jumped into the Benz riding off, knowing their actions was going to cause an all out war, one that neither knew how they were going to win, but both were ready and willing to ride or die for their act of Bogusness.

Weeks had passed and no one seemed to know what happened to Maurice. Many had their suspicions due to the fact that the content in the trunk was ten keys of heroin, leaving many of the local dealers drugless. Mysteriously, the powerful drug started to filter back into the streets: only the distributor wasn't the usual one who dispersed the drug. It was Dig a Hole who now controlled the flow of heroin in the city, at least for the time being.

Knowing that he had the only weight in the city he took full advantage and served it raw and damn near uncut. As a result he had every dope fiend north, south and even from St. Paul coming to his spot for their fix. The only way the other dealers were able to cop from him was to pay his prices, and they weren't cheap. In his mind, they deserved to be treated this way because they had no problem paying the out-of-town boys the ticket they charged, so why accept less?

Now having interactions with all the different gangs, Dig a Hole took advantage of the opportunity to watch and observe the various members of the opposing groups, knowing that it would only be a matter of time before everyone put it together that he was responsible for the stolen shipment and Maurice's death.

Recognizing this, he began to assemble his own click to not only distribute his drugs, but to literally take over the whole fucken city. After thoroughly thinking out his plans he set forth the action to make them a reality.

Because he was from Minnesota he was pretty familiar with the other people from various gangs. Already knowing the riders, he started recruiting them individually with the lure of his riches and the chance to do what they wanted, how they wanted, and to whom they wanted.

After several tests he narrowed the group down to eight people ready to chase the fast cash by all means necessary. His team of eight niggas was ready to give the streets of Minneapolis the bizness! This was the start of how eight hood niggas took over an entire city.

P.O. Box 2112
Minneapolis, MN 55402
www.streetlifepublisherz.com

Available Now!

Get Down Or Lay Down By Derrick Johnson	$15.00
A Real Goon's Bible By Derrick Johnson	$15.00
Cut Throat Mafia By Derrick Johnson	$15.00
Murda Squad By Derrick Johnson	$15.00
Street Kingz By Derrick Johnson	$15.00
Crooked By Anthony Creach	$15.00
Supply And Demand By Javetta Taplette & Derrick Johnson	$15.00
Omerta By Larry Eat'em Up Brown	$15.00
Jealousy Breeds Envy By Robert Williams	$15.00
Jackerz By Cool Daddy Swag	$15.00

Coming Soon! 2015

Lay It Down By Derrick Johnson (Sequel To Get Down Or Lay Down)

Dangerous Minds By Wakinyan Wakan Mcarthur

Turned Out By Edward Robinson

Shattered But Not Broken By Lakesha Johnson

Jealousy Breeds Envy Trilogy By Robert Williams

Love Me Not A Collection Of Nightmares By Larie Lewis

(Shipping and handling is $3.99 for 1st book and $1.99 for each additional book. Acceptable forms of payment are money order or instituional checks ONLY. *All books are $13.99 for institutions.* FOR ONLINE PURCHASES LOG ONTO WWW. STREETLIFEPUBLISHERZ.COM. All orders are shipped within 36 hours from the time they reach the office and are sent confirmation delivery. If you need the status of your order, please email customer service at Derrick@streetlifepublisherz.com.

TOTAL $ _____

Purchaser Information

Name: _____

Reg. # _____

Address: _____

_____

_____

City:_____

State: _____   Zip: _____

Total number of books ordered: _____